THE NOBEL MAZE

From the discovery of insulin to that of stress

First Published in Great Britain 2018 by Mirador Publishing

Copyright © 2018 by William and Hélène Rostène

First edition: 2018

A copy of this work is available through the British Library.

ISBN: 978-1-912192-87-8

Mirador Publishing
10 Greenbrook Terrace
Taunton
Somerset
TA1 1UT

The Nobel Maze
From the discovery of insulin to that of stress

An historical novel by
William and Hélène Rostène

Original: Les Caprices du Nobel: A la découverte du diabète et du stress, éditions L'Harmattan, Paris, France

Translation from French by Alison L. Strayer

~ *DEDICATION* ~

The greatest joy in life is to accomplish. It is the getting not the having. It is the giving not the keeping.

Cameron Lecture, Sir Frederick Banting

All sciences are vain and full of errors that are not born of experience, the mother of all knowledge.

Leonardo Da Vinci Notebooks

~ PART ONE ~

~ *CHAPTER 1* ~

Summer, 1918
Northwest Front, France

"*Maman, Maman*, come get me!"

The young man had been crying out for hours. He was lying on a pile of bedding. Other beds were strewn pell-mell over the floor of the 'ward', the common room of a farmhouse behind the front lines. All around this makeshift hospital for British soldiers, the Somme Valley lay devastated by artillery bombardment.

The duty nurse was mystified by the delirious young man. She had no idea what regiment he was from, or why he screamed so loudly, and in French. A local farmer had brought him on a cart and laid him in front of the hospital, or what was left of it. The soldier had no papers, no dog tag or helmet, only civilian clothes that were far too big for him and an armband with a red cross on it. It was the kind worn by the stretcher-bearers who transported the wounded from the trenches. The nurse approached the surgeon, who was finishing a dressing.

"Dr. Banting, do you have a moment?" she said. "A young man was brought in. He's been delirious since he arrived. He speaks French and always says the same thing. It's not hard to understand. He's calling for his mother. We were waiting for you to examine him, but I know you've been operating on soldiers all morning. Would you like something to drink?"

"Thank you, Judith I'll join you in a minute."

The last few days had brought a steady stream of wounded whose injuries were increasingly severe. The situation was critical.

Banting said, "If this continues, we'll have nothing to run the hospital with. The High Command will have to be informed."

The regular explosions of shells could be heard in the distance. Yet the front lines were several kilometres away. The electricity often had to be restored, and at the hospital they wondered how they still had any at all.

Judith circulated among the wounded, stopping at every bed. She spoke to them gently, hoping to bring them comfort. Before the war, she had worked as a nurse on the outskirts of London. She liked listening to Dr. Banting talk. She loved his Canadian accent, the strange words that people never used in England. They made her laugh sometimes, despite the tragic circumstances.

Hours passed and finally Dr. Banting emerged from surgery. He came to see the wounded that had most recently arrived.

"Have you examined him?"

"Yes, he has shrapnel in his left leg, but it doesn't look very deep."

"I'll take a look. Bring him into the other room, please, Judith."

A quick examination revealed the scraps of metal embedded in the young man's leg and hip. They had to be removed before infection set in. It was not until midnight that the patient, still unconscious, could be returned to bed. Judith and Dr. Banting continued to wonder what a French soldier was doing behind British lines. Why the armband and the civilian clothes? Was he a spy? The next three days brought no clues, as the young soldier only continued to call for his mother.

"*Maman*, come take me home!"

The only change was that he was delirious in English now. Judith and Dr. Banting came and went, checking on him regularly. They wondered where he could possibly be from. With his childlike features, he couldn't be more than twenty. After a week, his main wounds began to heal with no sign of infection. One morning, he began to stir, and then slowly opened his eyes. He gazed at a ray of light from the skylight on the red brick wall.

"*Maman*, come... Where am I?" he cried, waking men in the other beds. "Is anyone there? What is this place? What am I doing here?"

The duty nurse hurried to fetch Judith and Dr. Banting, who had told her to summon them if anything changed. Luckily, Dr. Banting was not operating that day, but writing reports on earlier surgeries. He rushed to the young man's bed. The patient looked at him in a familiar way. Clearly he had no fear of white coats.

"You were lucky," said Dr. Banting.

"What do you mean, lucky?" the young man replied.

"The shrapnel you got could have severed the femoral vein and made you lose your leg... or your life."

The young man listened in silence. Calmly, Dr. Banting explained how the farmer had found him unconscious behind the front line trenches, and brought him to the field hospital. The doctor was waiting for the right moment to ask his burning question. He didn't want to startle the young man.

"Do you know where we are?"

"Not a clue."

"In France. The Somme to be exact."

"Filthy trenches full of putrefaction and death. How d'you save all those poor men from disease, and most of all from human stupidity? Fighting to win a mile of land that is lost the next day! When you think of all the vast spaces there are on this Earth, vast territories where nobody wants to go because of all the dangerous beasts, but one day man will conquer…"

"Let me take your pulse and temperature. Try to rest. We'll continue this conversation later."

Frustrated, Dr. Banting decided he should wait to ask his question. In his opinion, the young man was delirious, though he did not have a high temperature. For now, it was better to leave him be.

"I don't understand," he said to Judith. "Our young man speaks both French and English, says perfectly sensible things except when he starts going on about vast spaces, and that we're trapped here in unspeakable chaos, and nothing has changed for months…"

"Very strange, indeed," Judith replied, frowning.

~ *CHAPTER 2* ~

Dr. Banting hadn't slept for days. Despite the help and goodwill of his assistants, he couldn't cope with the continuous influx of wounded soldiers. Some were dead on arrival, asphyxiated by the foul battlefield gases that permeated the air for miles around. Other men had been torn to shreds by shells that exploded out of nowhere. Exhausted, eyes bloodshot, all that the doctor hoped for was a little peace and quiet, a few minutes' rest before resuming his gruelling and often futile work. But his rest, in a cramped room, never lasted long.

"Dr. Banting, that young man from who-knows-where tried to get up but collapsed next to his bed. Nothing serious, fortunately, but he's very agitated. He asked to see you. I told him it's impossible, that you have too much work."

"I'll go for a few moments, Judith, I'm just as curious as you are."

They passed through a series of rooms, some extensions of the sprawling farmhouse, or outbuildings with canvas tarps stretched over the top. All that could be heard were groans and unrelenting cries of pain. Drugs were starting to run out, and every day Dr. Banting fervently hoped for an end to the massacre. He approached the bed where the young man had been tied down. He began to speak to him softly in English.

"Don't worry, you'll pull through. A little patience and all will be well."

"Who are you?" the young man replied sharply.

"Dr. Banting, Frederick Banting. I'm the head physician here. We're in a field hospital for British forces. Who are you? Where are you from?"

"I don't know what I'm doing here, I don't remember anything. I've never seen you before. Why am I in a hospital in England?"

"You're not in England; you're in France, in the Somme."

"But why are you speaking to me in English if I'm in France?"

Dr. Banting was taken aback and more confused than ever.

"What's your name?"

A long silence.

"Please go. I'm very tired."

Dr. Banting understood. They were not to insist. Though he yearned to know where the man came from, they would have to be patient. The young fellow would eventually talk to him.

He had to wait a little longer. Then one day, he looked up and there the young man was, standing before him, leaning on a crutch he'd somehow concocted. He'd hobbled to the room where he expected Dr. Banting to be.

The doctor was raising a steaming cup to his mouth and holding a cigarette.

"What a surprise! Can I offer you a cup of tea? It's not very good, but we have to make do with what we've got. You look as if you're doing much better, just as I predicted the other day."

"I wanted to thank you for what you did for me. I'm young. I hope I'll get the use of my leg again. I don't want to limp for my whole life. I don't want people, especially girls, taking pity on me."

"Don't worry, once the wounds heal you'll be as good as new. What's your name?" Dr. Banting really wanted to know.

"Paul Dormont."

"So you're French, that's what I thought. What were you doing in the British battalions?"

"You're half wrong, Doctor."

"What do you mean 'half'?"

"My father's French, or was French, hence my name. My mother's Irish, I mean, was Irish."

"It's all a little confusing. So that's why you speak two languages?"

"Something like that."

"Thanks for telling me your name. But my question hasn't been answered."

"Actually... I'm Australian. My parents became Australian too, like all immigrants. I come from Melbourne. I was under the command of General John Monash. Do you know him?"

"No, I've never heard of him."

"That's a shame. He's an extraordinary man. It is because of him or for him, that I'm here... in France, I mean. I've been here since the Dardanelles, where we suffered in battle with the Turks. In truth, we had to withdraw to save lives. At Gallipoli, there were just 12,000 of us Anzacs, facing 40,000 Turks on a hill. What could we do, poorly equipped in a country we didn't know? The battle was badly planned. It wasn't the fault of Monash, who was only commanding an Australian brigade at the time. The fault lay with the English generals. They probably thought of those soldiers from around the world, 'from the colonies', as nothing more than cannon fodder. I'd just arrived from Australia but was still too young to serve, so I was drafted into a medical unit in Egypt that treated the wounded from the Dardanelles. Also, the ones who'd caught all kinds of diseases, dysentery, gastric and respiratory problems, and others they'd contracted in Cairo's brothels. All under a blazing sun and swarms of flies."

"You seem to know something about medicine."

"From my parents, who are both doctors. Things I've heard around home since I was little."

Dr. Banting finally asked his question.

"Why were you wearing a red cross on your arm like a medic or stretcher-bearer? You were in civilian clothes, without a dog tag or regiment number."

"I can only answer part of your question. The red cross on my armband is because I'm a stretcher-bearer in the 3rd Australian division under General Monash. We arrived in France in June of last year and shortly after we fought in Flanders, Messines, Ypres and Passchendaele. About my clothes and regiment number, I have no idea where they went. The French peasant who brought me here probably gave me his clothes and took my uniform. I don't know why."

"I have to go now; I've still got a lot of work to do. But I hope we'll get to talk again."

"And what about you, where are you from?"

"I'm Canadian."

"That's the back of beyond!"

"Depends on your point of view, I guess... for an Australian, maybe so." It was the first time in many months that Dr. Banting had laughed so heartily.

~ *CHAPTER 3* ~

Paul had been at the field hospital for a month. He had come to know the place and the people in it. He couldn't help thinking he was lucky to have got away unscathed, although his leg was still very painful. When he saw some of his cronies, as young as he but crippled for life, he told himself that war was a disgusting thing and hoped this one was the last. But in his heart he doubted it.

The day before, Paul had gone out to take the air for the first time. Why did his eyes fill with tears? Because he felt free again? Because he could walk? He wept just contemplating the devastated landscape. Not a single living tree only charred branches. In the distance, the remains of a farm; toppling stonewalls, black as the surrounding atmosphere. No animals, no birds, nothing. This was not how he had imagined France the France his father had told him so much about when he was a child. He'd told him about Paris, which he loved passionately.

His parents hadn't heard from him for a long time. They were no doubt waiting dejectedly in Melbourne, though it was a haven of peace and quiet.

Paul was lost in thought when he sensed someone behind him.

"You're quite an early bird, Paul," Judith said in the soft voice he'd heard beneath consciousness when they first brought him to hospital.

"I was looking at this disaster. This beautiful country. Will this be the image of France I'll carry around forever? I'd have liked to go to Paris, but that's impossible."

"You have your whole life to go to Paris."

"Do you think that's easy when you live in Australia? It's at the ends of the Earth." Judith smiled.

"Paul, I've been here almost a year and I've never been back to England. So you can understand that Paris... is only a dream."

"Judith, do we have any news about what's really happening? I know the information from the High Command must be false. They have to keep the troops' spirits up."

"The situation must be about the same, but the noise of shelling seems a little fainter. We're not so far from Amiens and maybe from the end of the war, too. It seems our commanders have decided to change strategy and attack quickly, in small groups with tanks and Lewis guns, which are supposed to be more efficient. And in good weather."

Paul knew about the new strategy, the work of John Monash. Was it really possible that he had won the others over to his side? Persuaded the English staff they had to put an end to trench warfare, which led to nothing but a growing number of victims?

"It's true. Fortunately, it isn't too hot in the summer in the north of France. As a matter of fact, Paul, we found your battalion and superiors near Hamel, not far from here. We described your condition and they've decided to send you back to Australia as soon as possible. You'll be leaving here, and I'm happy for you. I'm sure Dr. Banting wants to see you before you go. I think he quite likes you. He appreciates the stretcher-bearers and nurses who dedicate their lives to saving others. See you later, I must get back."

Paul could not bring himself to go back inside, despite the odour of gas outside—pungent, penetrating, and a fact of everyday life now—and the light rain beginning to fall. He thought of the future. What future could there be for the world? And how could he return to Australia while the war raged on and the seas were so dangerous? He startled at the sound of a truck bringing new wounded men, and turned to watch the unfortunates who would probably never see their families again. Dealing with death had hardened him. He was no longer the happy adolescent who left Melbourne to follow Monash and the Australian troops.

Forgetting his injury, he gripped the side of a stretcher with both hands. As he was helping to carry the stretcher inside, he passed Banting.

"I see things are going much better and you have recovered your strength. I hope to find some time to talk before you leave, but we can't be sure of anything here."

Paul thought, *Well, well, Dr. Banting is talking to me almost like a friend—me, Paul Dormont. Not too surprising. I've just gone from the status of patient to that of stretcher-bearer. From unconscious to conscious.*

He went back to his bed to pack his things. Except that he had nothing to pack. It made him laugh. No suitcase, no clothes, only toiletries the hospital had given him. A book, a single book on a dusty shelf. He reached for it. He needed to give it a hard shake before he could see the title, embossed in gold: *Les Fables de La Fontaine*.

What was the book doing there? he wondered. A book in French. Probably left behind when the farm was converted into a hospital. He lay down with his eyes full of tears. The book brought back memories from childhood. His father had read him the very same fables. With no hesitation he began reciting *The Raven and the Fox*. Even just listening to the verse's melody, without really understanding the meaning, carried him off to the world of children, and he fell asleep, calm and happy.

"Paul, wake up! Dr. Banting wants to see you."

A swift return to reality, where the rooms smelled of blood and tobacco smoke.

"Thank you, Paul, for your help with the stretchers. I see you feel better. Be careful though, your wound isn't fully healed. We've received the order to return you to a fortified camp of Australian troops not far from here, in Corbie. I hope this war will be over soon. I can't take any more. Yet I've only been here a few months. You know, like you, I wanted to sign up when the war began. They didn't want me because I wear glasses. Maybe they thought I'd lose them on the battlefield. A blessing in disguise, because I was able to keep on at medical school in Toronto."

"Toronto? Where's that?"

"In Ontario, Canada, near the Great Lakes. Does that ring a bell? Winters are harsh, with a lot of snow, like almost everywhere in the country. I've been told my country is somewhat similar to yours."

"Not the climate, apparently. In Melbourne, even in winter, it never gets very cold."

"I wasn't referring to the climate but the people. A country of immigrants, mostly from Europe, like your parents, as you told me the other day. Canadians, Australians, all members of the Commonwealth. Which, unfortunately, is probably why we're here."

"It's true; it can't be easy, deciding to leave your country and go to live somewhere else. As I told you, my father's a doctor, a neurologist. He teaches at the University of Melbourne and works on Parkinson's disease. My mother started out as a nurse then became a doctor too. I love my parents. I'm full of admiration for them and what they do. For you, too, come to that. For helping people who are suffering. Maybe that's why I committed to being a medic. I was too young to go to medical school."

"Paul, if you can, go to medical school. It's a wonderful profession, despite the constraints and sacrifices it requires. As you can see, in medicine, we don't only heal the sick, we reassure people. We give people hope and discover unknown areas. I trained in orthopaedics, which isn't much use here... Well... I guess you're leaving tomorrow, Paul. Maybe one day our paths will cross again."

They now had to say goodbye, one man unaware of the glorious destiny that awaited him, the other determined to start medical school upon his return to his native country.

~ *CHAPTER 4* ~

The dream I had had in that isolated camp behind the front lines was going to come true.

I was on my way to Melbourne and had just learned that, on that particular July 4, 1918, General John Monash, in Hamel, with the support of the Australian and New Zealand forces, had won his first major victory. With the strategy of small groups that he had perfected and set in motion, the German enemy had been beaten in less than two hours. It was a stunning success that paved the way to the north and the Hindenburg Line.

British High Command was forced to admit that Monash and his "small-scale well-prepared advances," as he put it, with Anzac troops, had just scored a crucial point. The situation that had remained at a standstill since the Battle of the Somme in 1916 could now be altered.

Spirits were rising among the troops. Everyone enjoyed quiet moments away from the trenches before returning to battle or home.

The freedom train was taking me to Marseilles. You would never have thought we were at war. Marseilles had also changed since our battalion had landed in its port, two years earlier. The people in the streets were mostly women, elegant and smiling at passing soldiers, who had eyes only for them. Some men with the accent of the south of France were involved in a heated discussion of the situation. They were reading papers around a half-empty bottle of anisette, the summer heat making their thirst acute. I started listening to them from a nearby bench.

They called out to me:

"What're you doing all alone there, soldier? Come join us, we're celebrating the advance of the Allied troops on the Front!"

Such an invitation could not be refused, an opportunity to finally meet real French people.

"You know, we don't speak English, but everyone knows we owe you a debt of gratitude."

I had never heard the expression before.

"You don't understand, I'm sure, but come here so we can give you a kiss. We love all the soldiers who helped deliver our country from those dirty Boches."

I knew the French kissed each other at the drop of a hat. It was a custom, and a habit that my parents had never lost.

"Would you look at that, a Brit who lets you kiss him! Kid, you're too young to have gone to war. I'm sure your parents are waiting on the other side of the sea – not our good sea, the big one. But you don't understand what I'm saying, do you? Come on, have a drink."

"Actually, I understand you very well. Thank you, I will be happy to have a drink with you, even if I don't know anything about this drink."

"You speak French so well and don't know *anisette*? We're going to have to do something about that! Especially in August, on a scorcher like today!"

They were amazed that I spoke French. I told them about

the trenches and our victories in Flanders and the Somme. The next day, I remembered nothing of what was said except that our troops had managed to break through German lines to Amiens and quickly advance towards the Hindenburg Line that stretched thirty kilometres between Cambrai and St. Quentin. I also remembered sitting drunk and happy between two large gunny sacks, facing the boats that were loaded with food and equipment for the repatriation of the Anzac troops.

Our boat was comfortable. At least, that's the impression I had after months in the trenches with mud, rats, putrid odours and thick fog. I was lucky. A cruise ship, the *Osmonde,* had been chartered to bring us back home. The British fleet was definitely missing boats. My first shower was an intense pleasure. I would have spent hours in there if my wound hadn't started to sting under the hot spray. I was also ravenous; it had been two days since I had eaten anything.

No noise. Only the lapping of water and the cables knocking against each other. At last some quiet, which my ears had forgotten about. I dreamed it was the previous century and I was making my parents' journey from Europe to settle in Australia. Stories from this trip had been told to me right from the cradle. I saw myself sitting at the coffee table in the living room in front of an atlas, examining the line drawn in red ink showing the long journey, which eventually led to my birth in Melbourne. I saw the Mediterranean, the Suez Canal and the long Pacific crossing before they reached the west coast and finally the south of Australia.

Just at that moment, I began to sweat, burning hot all of a sudden, a lump in my throat. I cried out and sat up in bed, shaking. My neighbours were wakened by my cries.

"It's nothing, don't worry, probably a nightmare."

"It happens to all of us who were in the trenches. And it's probably just the start."

I couldn't tell them it wasn't a memory of the trenches but panic and terror that the ship would go down. Mingled in my mind were the possible attack on our ship by a German submarine and my grandfather's tragic death in a shipwreck on the southern coast of Australia before he was able to reach my country. I'd heard so much about my grandfather, a brilliant scientist that I had the impression that he was there with me, taking that trip again.

My fear began to fade. I quickly dressed and hurried to the deck. The sea air made me feel better. I opened my eyes and then I saw it. There before me was the coast, and a chain of majestic mountains. I smelled an unknown, fine and gentle scent, a mixture of different essences.

"Corsica," said a sailor as he passed. "It is called the Island of Beauty. Too bad we aren't stopping there. You're right to stay on the deck. Morning is the most pleasant time. And the sun rising behind the mountains – so beautiful!"

He disappeared before I could reply and tell him how much I shared his opinion. I could not move. I savoured those moments of solitude and silent contemplation, facing that bright island.

~ *CHAPTER 5* ~

Was it true what they'd said at the port of Marseilles? Had our troops really advanced? Would the war finally end? We had been without news for the entire three weeks we had been at sea. Another week and we'd be able to see the Australian coast. My fear of our boat being torpedoed faded as we left the combat zones. I gradually resumed my activities with the injured and the sick, bringing what relief I could to those in need. The weather was cooler now, for it was winter in the southern hemisphere.

There are moments in life that we envisage before we live them. They never go quite as imagined. I wondered how it would be to see my parents again. Had they changed? They must have had news of me by now; the High Command had surely sent word of my repatriation. I was just hoping they had received my letter, in which I told them that I was only slightly injured.

Luckily the weather was fine and the sea calm for our passage through Cape Otway, where my grandfather perished. When we passed the high and majestic cliffs of southern Australia, I felt none of the anxiety I had dreaded. Crowds gathered on the docks of Port Melbourne where the *Osmonde* was preparing to cast anchor. A multitude of little Australian flags welcomed the 'diggers'. There they were, searching the crowd, my father going grey and my mother still beautiful, resplendent in her floral dress. As for the diggers', all of us had a single goal: to enjoy a normal life after years of hell. For many of us that might prove difficult, but we had to live again. Probably not as we had before – we had been so young when we left. We had become grown men, maybe too quickly.

Throughout the first week after my return, I did not want to do anything except find my bearings and familiar objects. My parents never questioned me. As medical professionals, they knew very well that things would emerge of their own accord. They just asked about Monash – Jack, as he was called by his friends, including my parents. The last time I had seen the general was in early July at his headquarters in the Château de Bertangles, near Amiens. That day we had received a visit from Prime Minister Billy Hughes, accompanied by the Commander-in-Chief Douglas Haig. They reviewed the troops and Monash made a long speech that roused our enthusiasm, reminding us how we could advance on the German lines with our tanks and aircraft as offensive weapons. He had lost weight, but seemed to be in good enough shape despite the years of combat.

"Did he tell you anything about his wife's health?" was the first question my mother asked.

"Yes, he talked to me about Vic when we were in Egypt. He had a message from Melbourne, maybe from you, saying she was seriously ill. The whole contingent knew that his spells of exhaustion had to do with her illness. How is she?"

"She's not too bad but I don't know what the future holds."

"And what about their daughter Bertha?" I inquired.

"Bertha is wonderful. She doesn't want it known that her father's a general. She still works as a nurse here in Melbourne and she's got a lot of work, as you can imagine."

"I'll go see her soon."

"I think she'd be very happy to see you," my father said, pleased that I was starting to take an interest in life again.

"I'm going to get the papers. I'm anxious to see what's happening."

"It seems the news is good, but with journalists... you always wonder if they're telling the truth. Politicians are no better. I don't really like that Hughes, you know."

"I think Monash agrees."

So there I was, back in Melbourne. It hadn't changed much. Very quiet, after the battlefield; still a small provincial town. A nice place to live, with friends all around you. Few people in the streets, faces impenetrable. I suspected that everyone had a family member at the Front and was waiting for news. Surely they were also thinking how privileged I was to be there, to have somehow escaped the war. I wanted to cry out that they were mistaken, that I had fought and was injured. It was the eyes of women that disturbed me most of all. I felt they resented me for being there. True, there were very few men in the street. Older children worked in factories and children were in school at that time of day.

Displayed in front of the newspaper stand were the two major dailies, *The Age* and *The Argus*, with at least one headline in common: 'Advance of Australian and Canadian Corps on the Western Front in France'. I bought both and asked if they still had papers from the previous weeks. Sitting quietly in Victoria Park, I read the details of the Battle of Amiens in August, and the comments on the rapid response of our troops. I recognised the strategy developed by Monash. A column in one of the papers described King George V's visit to Bertangles and the knighting of General John Monash Commander of the Order of the Bath.

Articles from late August 1918 described the taking of Mont St. Quentin and Peronne, the last bases before the Hindenburg Line, with a minimum of casualties. Then there was an entire page with a speech by Monash, including two sentences that seized my attention: 'We have changed the course of the war. Now we can get out of this dirty war, quickly'. The articles not only emphasised his leadership in battle but also his engineering skills, with the rehabilitation of the Peronne railway line for the transport of troops and equipment, particularly those provided by the Americans. Bridge reconstruction was another example of his experience in Melbourne before the war where he had worked on the Yarra River. 'We need to rebuild and retool for the pursuit and final defeat of the Germans. All that, before another winter is upon us'.

Over the autumn of 1918, a large stack of papers accumulated in my room, so much so that it became almost impossible to enter. More and more articles were written in praise of Australian soldiers and their leader. The war correspondents Keith Murdoch and Charles Bean, who had not been kind to Monash since Gallipoli, had to face facts. Even the English papers had got in on the act; their journalists were amazed by the man's charm and pragmatism, his calm and well-chosen words that nonetheless left no doubt as to his hatred of the war, its absurdity and horror, its destruction of an entire generation. One of those journalists, Arthur Conan Doyle, even wrote that Monash was the greatest general he had met at the Front.

I closely followed the progress of the Allied troops on a detailed map of the Somme that I had found in one of my pockets, no doubt put there by one of my mates at the Marseilles bistro.

~ *CHAPTER 6* ~

Two months had passed since my return. Nothing interested me so much as following the development of the situation in Europe. I sometimes regretted not being with them, especially since the advance of our troops had been spectacular. The Hindenburg Line of German defence, eighteen kilometres long, had been swept away by the 1st and 4th divisions. The English press recognised the Australians' extraordinary motivation; recognised that the victories since the battle of Hamel were mainly the work of our forces, commanded by John Monash. Our forces led the combat, even against the advice of Prime Minister Billy Hughes, who thought that his country's troops had given enough in the last months of the war. But now, so close to their goal, the Australian soldiers were too proud to agree to anything that might have obscured their great contribution to final victory. It happened very suddenly. Prince Max von Baden requested an immediate armistice on October 5th. However, they had to wait another month for the Germans to retreat from Lens, Armentieres and Lille.

The newspapers laboured for the entire night of November 11 to announce the news on the front page of *The Age* and *The*

Argus. The war was over. Monash had no more orders to give his troops. Nor did he have to take any more orders from the English, the politicians or Australian journalists.

Repatriation began. Which of my companions would return? How many remained on French soil? Whenever I heard the horns of ships approaching the port of Melbourne, I ran down to the dock hoping to see familiar faces.

It was Burnet I saw first, standing on the deck of a boat from Marseilles. He was easy to recognise; he always wore a big smile, even at the most difficult of times, when we had to run under shellfire with our stretcher to bring back the wounded. Despite my desire to be the first to go and throw my arms around him, I waited to see if anyone else was waiting for him. As he reached the bottom of the gangway, a girl with blonde hair rushed to him and kissed him passionately. Then a young man, a little younger than me, I thought, moved forward to embrace him.

There were so many people on the docks, as there were always boats arriving from France. I quickly lost sight of them. I only remembered that Burnet did not live in Melbourne.

The following weeks were punctuated by the arrival of boats. It became habit for Melbourne residents to rush to the port as soon as an arrival was announced. Sadly, some were losing hope, for their loved ones were not among the passengers. I had decided to break with the past that had laid waste to my youth – to resume living, retrieve hope, and have fun. At the time I had left, I was too young to have a girlfriend to wait for me, throw her arms around me, passionately kiss me on my return, or make love with me. The war had stolen the best years of my life. I had to make up for lost time.

The only women I knew were my mother and Bertha. It was

because of Bertha, perhaps, that I joined the army to follow her father. Yes, Bertha Monash, four years older than me. I had watched her with interest when I was young. When I left, in my adolescent eyes she was already a real woman, untouchable, inaccessible. Even now I was jealous of her. Not because of the men she met, whose names I never knew, except for Gersh, but for another reason. She knew Paris, she visited London. At seventeen, she had attended the funeral of Edward VII and the coronation of George V, but that didn't interest me. On the other hand, she had seen Paris, the Eiffel Tower, lunched at a cafe on the Boulevard Montparnasse, dined at Maxim's, while I, of French descent, had not even got close to seeing the city. It exasperated me no end. The field hospital had only been a hundred kilometres from Paris. She planned to return, on her father's request, to visit the sites of our feats of arms – ours, the poor soldiers'! I couldn't bear it! She didn't understand why I pushed her away when she asked me to talk about her father, and the war, and France. I did not dare tell her that I was jealous, that I would have liked to go with her. However, I now had to think of myself, enjoy the present moment and look ahead to my future.

I did not have to torment myself for long. University beckoned. Medical school anyway. I had wanted to be a doctor when I was just a stretcher-bearer. I wanted to help people as I had in the trenches. The face and the words of Dr. Banting came back to my mind. What had become of him? He had no doubt returned to Canada, been reunited with his family, maybe his wife, although he had never mentioned being married.

I fell asleep on the couch and dreamed of Canada, imagining it a little like Australia, with kangaroos jumping in the vast white expanses, and emus that could not reach their heads out of the snow.

"Wake up, Paul. It's registration day at the university," my mother said.

"Where am I? I was having a dream."

"An interesting one, I hope?"

"I don't know..."

The University of Melbourne was not far. I decided to walk.

Registration was no problem. It was enough to say that you'd been in the war, and they handed you a sheet to fill in for free tuition. I had no special privileges, even though my father still occasionally taught neuroanatomy at the medical school.

"You haven't filled the form in properly, sir," said an employee in an unfriendly tone of voice.

"I wrote my last name, first name and date of birth."

"That is not an English name... Dormont."

"So, it's an embarrassment not to be called Smith – like you, I suppose?"

"I won't stand for this, young man!"

"Nor I, sir."

"How dare you? I refuse to enrol you!"

That was too much. I grasped the man by the collar of his jacket and hoisted him from his chair, which noisily fell to the floor. He tried to fight back. I rolled off a punch that knocked him flat. He held his nose, blood running through his fingers.

"Excuse me, I didn't mean to do that."

Instinctively I leapt into my wartime role of medic.

"Let me look at your nose. Lean forward!"

He was red with anger, but his nose was not broken.

"I didn't mean to hurt you, but you insulted me."

"It is you who insulted me!"

"So why the reference to my name?"

"I once had a Dr. Dormont. He saved my wife several years ago. He shouldn't have... she left me."

"But he was only doing his duty."

"That's true, but then she ruined my life."

"And that's why you're angry with me?"

"Yes."

"That's not a very good reason… even though Dr. Dormont is my father!"

We left it at that. I treated the wound and he enrolled me.

Of course, the story got around. The following week, in my very first class, I alrcady had a reputation. Between 'the boxer' and 'Mr. Fearless', not to speak of my military past, I was either rejected or admired, especially from the fairer sex, sadly underrepresented in our year. It was a class of about thirty, all younger than me. None of them had gone to the Front, being too young for the draft, or tried signing up before draft age, as I had done to follow John Monash.

Among my fellow students, I recognised the young man I had seen hugging my trench mate, Burnet.

~ *CHAPTER 7* ~

My four years of medical school went by very quickly, perhaps too quickly. I went from the status of student to that of worker in no time. Those were good years. I don't know why, but I found the study of medicine relatively easy. I worked at night, of course, but not always. I was intent on savouring the pleasures of life of which the war had deprived me. I accompanied my parents to concerts and the theatre, when they went with John's wife, Vic. I went mainly because John and Vic's daughter Bertha was there. She loved music. The two women were both musicians and played the piano beautifully.

Meanwhile, John Monash was back from the war, with all the honours a victorious general was due. George V had knighted him; the French and the Belgians had decorated him with the Military Cross. And yet throughout this period, he faced systematic opposition from Keith Murdoch, a journalist from the Front. The two men had hated each other since Monash had been given command. The reasons for this persistent hatred were unclear, but Murdoch and his colleague Charles Bean had always emphasised that Monash was of German origin and moreover Jewish. Even before the war, anti-Semitism was widespread. Murdoch and Bean had never been able to accept that a Jew, who according to them was pretentious, could be in command of the Australian troops. They also supported Prime Minister Billy Hughes, who feared that Monash would enter politics and due to his popularity, replace him. On the other hand, everyone who had gone to war had nothing but admiration for Monash.

He had become a revered figure. Since his return he had participated in all the public events, all the parades in the streets of Melbourne. At public speaking engagements, he held forth brilliantly about military actions and politics, and also religion and music. He became the personality that everyone wanted at his or her dinner table. To his surprise, he was offered the post of Director-General of Repatriation and Demobilization.

Despite all these claims on his time, he came to our home on a regular basis, about once a week, as he had done even before the war. He enjoyed my parents' culture and intelligence, the richness of their conversation. Under no circumstances would I have missed these evenings with Monash. He always came with Vic and sometimes Bertha, who talked to us about France, where both women had travelled that autumn. That is the way things were until Vic's disease took a sudden turn in early 1920. She died in February.

On one of these evenings, I don't remember why, I found myself alone with Monash in the garden.

"So, Paul, how is medical school? It mustn't be too difficult to treat patients here, considering the conditions we worked under at Gallipoli or the Somme."

"There's no comparison. I heard that you made a speech thanking our nurses and medics and the whole medical profession for their work during the war. They say you were remarkable. Was Lizette with you?"

"Ah, Lizette," he said with a sigh. "I'll tell you, but you must keep it secret. Without her I don't think I'd have made it through that god-awful war. You may not have been aware of it, but I sometimes went to London."

"I know. I tried several times to see you at the HQ of Château Bertangles, but they told me that you had gone. To London, to Paris... while I was stuck in the hole."

"With Lizette, I got my strength back. The French use the word 'maîtresse'. Lizette is a love from my youth, a childhood friend of Vic's. She never married; she moved to London. I was married to Vic and we had Bertha. But when I found myself alone in Europe and saw Lizette in London after so many years, something happened between us, you know?"

"I can guess."

"We wrote each other regularly. It restored my spirits. King George V took a shine to me so I often went to London. I took the opportunity to see Lizette. We went to the theatre, sometimes every day."

"And frolicked a little too, I'm sure!"

"Ah, that's your French blood talking."

"My father told me that when you were a student, you had no shortage of lady friends."

"Well of course not! Not you?"

"I… you know, I had a lot of catching up to do. Because of you, by the way. I didn't have much chance to kick up my heels in London and Paris."

"It almost sounds as if you resent me."

"A little, especially since I still haven't seen Paris and I'm very jealous that Bertha has."

"You're young; you have your whole life to see Paris. It's

so beautiful, you'll see! But it's getting chilly. Time to go in."

"Just another word, sir. You know, I enlisted to follow you! To me, Gallipoli will always remain a failure for our troops. We didn't win against the Turks, and how absurd for Churchill to insist on waiting till we got to Constantinople, as in the Crusades. But we didn't lose either, except men, alas. I got to see Egypt and the pyramids. That was my reward. But I didn't know what to expect in France. Did you know I'd been wounded in the Somme going to help our men? I ended up in a makeshift war hospital behind the Front. A Canadian doctor operated on my leg."

"Yes, your mother wrote me and I knew you'd been sent back home. Unfortunately, I couldn't see you."

"It's because of that doctor that I came through as well as I did!"

"I know. It doesn't keep you from chasing girls, from what I hear."

"You're right, sir, it is getting chilly. Let's go back in."

The conversation continued inside. Monash was inexhaustible on the subject of the battles of the Somme and how they were conducted. He always carried a map of the region showing their military operations. It was a memory we shared. He kept the cherished map in a leather portfolio.

"After the Battle of Hamel, the coup de grace for the Germans, there was Mount St. Quentin and the capture of the fortified town of Peronne. I was surprised by how quickly our divisions advanced. Every day we had to draw up new plans. I was pleased that these victories gave the troops confidence. You know how the Australians are: tough in battle. It seems the Germans were more afraid of us than they were of the English. Some distinguished themselves brilliantly. A certain

Cartwright singlehandedly defeated a German battery near Cléry. I wanted it to be said that the Australian army corps was the one that took the Hindenburg Line. Even those bastards Bean and Murdoch had to admit I was right, that the tactics were all good, the aviation, tanks, and speed of execution. A forty kilometre advance to the east in four months. Completely unheard of for the past five years! The British press talked a lot about it. And I met two excellent journalists, not like Bean and Murdoch, who wrote for the London newspapers. I even kept the newspaper clippings and their names – both called Arthur! – O'Connor and a certain Conan Doyle. Too bad they wrote that they were British victories!"

"Yes, I read the article by Conan Doyle, 'Monash, the greatest of all generals'." We both laughed.

Monash continued to talk. He possessed great powers of persuasion; he always found the right words to turn any situation to his advantage.

"I was given two hundred thousand men, counting the British corps of the 3rd and the 9th divisions. I was impressed by the line of trenches and fortifications constructed by the Germans, eighty kilometres long by nine kilometres deep. The trained engineer in me took in every detail. Innovation, efficient construction, but so unsightly, built in three months. I myself was surprised at the collapse of the German troops. They were probably afraid of the robust Australian reputation. In one week, the Hindenburg Line was behind us, with no significant losses and many Boche prisoners. Our last offensive was Montbrehain. I even built a makeshift bridge, like the first ones here on the Yarra River, you remember, Serge?" he said, turning to my father, who had dozed off, lulled by the story he'd heard so many times before. "We received a letter from

Prince Max von Baden asking for an armistice. I had to go to London."

"To see Lizette?"

"Among other things."

"You know, sir, I don't regret following you. I'm proud I enlisted out of admiration for the man to whom we owe our victory."

"An Australian, right under the noses of the English and French military, narrow-minded, rigid and I daresay incompetent!"

We'd never heard him talk like that. Had he understood in retrospect that the war could have ended much earlier, and with fewer victims? Had we made the right decisions before?

It was late and we were all tired. At the door, I had a word in parting with Monash.

"Instead of all those decorations, sir, you deserve other rewards, a prize, for example. 'In recognition of the man who put an end to a senseless war and brought us peace'."

~ *CHAPTER 8* ~

Everyone was talking about Monash. He was everywhere, on every Front, his 'diggers' behind him. And he himself spared no effort to help them continue their education or find work. He stood up to the British leaders, telling them firmly that it was out of the question to keep Australian occupation forces in Germany. That was his role as Director-General of Repatriation and Demobilization. He threw all his energy and enthusiasm into it, unlike Hughes, who thought only about future elections and feared Monash would run against him. Hughes would likely be beaten if the hero of the Somme entered politics. As for Murdoch and Bean, they continued to support Hughes. Besides, they were unaware that Monash as a military man, preferred to be with his men. For him, politics was incidental. However, he demanded and was granted an annual parade in London and Melbourne to celebrate the Anzac troops. There were five thousand of us the first year, ten thousand the second.

Frank Burnet, who was called Mac, short for MacFarlane, his second name, had become my closest friend since had been in the trenches together. He was a serious fellow, much more than me. However, one drunken night out, we stupidly bet on who would make the greater number of female conquests over the year. To improve our score, we had to look outside the faculty. However we were both madly in love with the same girl, Florence, Florence Reading. She was stunning, with her long hair, slender figure and small round breasts that she expertly showed off. We tried every stratagem to convince her to forget her books for one night and to join us.

Underhandedly I tried to use the advantage my family represented:

"Florence, if you don't understand the course on the brain, my father can help. He told me so. You could come to our place this evening, for example."

And that is how I won out over Mac. It was a bit unfair really, but... Mac and I loved each other. A faithful friend, he quickly got over his disappointment. He was an excellent dancer and it wasn't enough for him to go to pubs with me, he also loved to go to the dances that were organised every week. And, as a result, by the end of our first two years of medical school, his 'list' was far longer than mine.

"I'm with Florence, but you... congratulations! I don't have enough fingers on both hands to count your conquests. You win, I admit it. Bravo, Casanova."

It was the first of January. We celebrated not only the New Year but also the anniversary of Australian independence. I remembered that day. It was 1901 and, all of five years old, I could feel my parents' joy. Despite their status as new immigrants, they had worked for independence from England with Alfred Deakin.

"Mac, you know we're lucky to be among the first Australians, the real ones, who founded their own country?"

"Is that why you went to the war?"

"Maybe it was. In fact, I've never told you, but I think I saw you several times on the port for the return of our troops. I was like you. Every time a ship arrived, I watched for the return of one of my buddies from the trenches."

"It's true; I was waiting for my older brother. One day, it finally happened."

"And you threw your arms around him. You were with a blonde girl."

"Yes, that's my sister. There are seven children in our family. But how do you know all that?"

"I watched you in the crowd. You disappeared. I wanted to see your brother too. We were together in the Somme."

"No!"

"Yes, I recognised him right away."

"Why didn't you say so before?"

"You knew I was in France at the same time as your brother. It's not as if the Anzac battalions were all over France."

"I hadn't thought about it, actually."

"How is he?"

"Okay. He took over from my father as branch manager of the Colonial Bank in Terang, where the family still lives. You have to come one day. I'm sure it will make him very happy. And everyone knows you. And you're my friend, right?"

"Of course. You're mine too, right?"

I went to Terang. A weekend was not enough for me to say everything. I told him how lucky I was to have a friend as loyal as Mac. And how difficult it had been to go back to normal life in Melbourne. On that visit I also learned that Mac was fascinated by insects and that when he was younger, he caught and collected them.

They called us for lunch. The barbecue was ready in the garden.

Mac's sister was lovely. But I was not about to woo her while I was still with Florence. Besides, she was engaged, from what I was told. She would make the man very happy, no doubt about that!

Back in Melbourne there was a delicate situation to be dealt with. Under pressure from Monash, Lizette had arrived from London. It was my father who went to meet her boat, as Monash had to remain as inconspicuous as possible. But Bertha found out and reacted very badly. I tried to reason with her, but she flatly refused to allow Lizette to move into the house where she lived with her father and her future husband, Gersh. She finally won out. She told her father that she would no longer see him if Lizette came to live with him. That was mere blackmail. Monash was crushed by his argument with Bertha. My father tried to console him as best he could, but nothing helped. A man can conquer the Hindenburg Line and capitulate to his own daughter.

The war was over now. Monash had to move on. A proposal to develop the Melbourne power grid gave him an opportunity to do so. He returned to his work as an engineer – and he was an expert. No more petty politics. He had achieved almost everything: honours, medals and recognition. Now over fifty-five, he had to think of himself and of what he had always liked to do: invent, build and create. He quickly understood why the local production was insufficient; the coal in the region was too wet. Ironically, the solution came from Germany, Halle in Zeitz Co. He had to hire Germans to supervise the facility that had to be established in Melbourne.

In April 1921, Bertha married Gersh, a dentist she had known for a long time. They left for Iona, but Lizette did not seize the opportunity to join John. She moved into a hotel room in Melbourne. The war was slowly receding into the past. Bertha, my childhood sweetheart, was married to another man. My youth was fading, too.

~ *CHAPTER 9* ~

"So what option did you choose?"

"At the risk of disappointing you, Father, I intend to follow in your footsteps. Neurology appeals to me."

"You could have found something else!"

"Maybe, but it fascinates me. We still know very little about brain disease, mental or degenerative... despite your work."

"The search never ends. Each of us brings his stone to the construction of ideas, and I hope one day this will help us understand how our brain works. If I had to do it all over again, well, you see, you're right, I'd do the same thing. But there are far more destructive diseases than shell shock that urgently need research. Think of the devastation caused by epidemics. Typhus in the Dardanelles, dysentery and cholera in the trenches. The French, with the Pasteur School, have contributed a great deal, but there's still so much to do to overcome these bacilli."

He was probably right, but we do not always know why we are attracted to one field and not another. I still had a few weeks to make up my mind.

Eventually, a letter arrived which decided my future.

A missive from the Ministry of War was delivered to my

parents' address. It was quite big. Naturally, they did not open it but they were intrigued. It is easy to imagine the scene, me carefully opening the letter as my parents looked on, waiting to hear what was in it.

War Ministry
Attention: Paul Dormont

Dear Sir,

Like many thousands of Australians, you have done a great deal to save our country and our democracy from the German yoke. Your service record, your courage and the dedication you have shown for helping your fellow citizens in those difficult times has led the War Minister to award you the Military Cross. It will be presented at a reception by General John Monash, who led the expeditionary force of which you were a member.

Please find attached the list of previous recipients of this award for all British troops.

With our congratulations,
For the Minister of War

John Monash must have had something do with this honour. My father took out a bottle of Bordeaux that he had preciously saved for a special occasion.

A few days later, during a shift at the hospital, I began to leaf through the long list of medal recipients, classified by country and alphabetically. A name jumped out at me: Captain Frederick Banting of London, Ontario.

I could not wait. I had to write to him. I needed to know how he had survived that horrible war, and what had become of him, if he was still a surgeon, and I also wanted to thank him for what he had done for me.

Australia is far from everything. I could not expect a response for two or three months. Alas my letter was returned to me, *'Unknown at this address'*. What an idiot! *'London'*. In my excitement of the moment, I wrote only *'London'*. How could a postman, even the best there is, find a doctor by the name of Banting in a city like London, with such a vague address? What's more, in my haste, I had not specified London, Ontario, Canada. I simply wrote *'London'*, and the letter had gone to England!

I resumed my letter writing, making a few changes. I wrote that I had followed his advice and was going to be a doctor... a neurologist. This time, I carefully checked the address and sent the letter off again.

It was early 1922 when I finally received a response from the University of Toronto.

Dear Paul,

What a joy to hear from you! I am glad to know you're in the peak of health and your wound just a bad memory. Do you know that I too was wounded on the Somme a few weeks after you left? It was late September and I was going to help wounded soldiers near Cambrai. In my case it was my arm that was hit by shrapnel, but fortunately it was less serious than I had first thought. In short, since my return, I have been a resident at the Toronto Hospital for Sick Children and then an assistant at the University of Western Ontario. I tried to settle in London, close to my family, as a general practitioner, but without success. However, as I didn't have many patients, I had lots of time to read, and one day I came across an excellent article by Moses Barron published in the Journal of Surgery, Gynaecology and Obstetrics. You can probably find it in Melbourne, too, and I highly recommend you read up on pancreatic surgery and its possible link with that terrible disease, diabetes. I know this is far removed from your field, but I would like to have your opinion. I was so impressed that I decided to concentrate on the treatment of this disease. I contacted a specialist in the carbohydrate metabolism, Prof. John McLeod at the University of Toronto. I'd been told to contact him about using his laboratory to practise surgery on dogs, as of course I was unable to do it anywhere else. Professor McLeod, I must say, did not take me very seriously, and I don't think he found my ideas about the pancreas interesting. But that's nothing new, and we'll see what comes of it. I recruited a young science student named Charles Best, who seems quite brilliant, and whom I can't even pay for this work. Doing medical research on top of clinical work is very rewarding but it naturally requires sacrifices, especially in terms of family life.

But enough said. How's medicine in Australia? Neurology is a vast field, still in its infancy. I am very pleased to hear that you have been given the Military Cross. That Monash you told me so much about must have had something to do with it. I recently learned that it is thanks to him that the war ended and we could finally leave the trenches.

Dear Paul, I hope we can continue this correspondence and keep each other informed about the latest developments in our respective fields.

Sincerely yours,

Dr. Frederick Banting

Dr. Banting did keep me informed of his discoveries, which were all the more surprising for having been made in a very short time. The exchange of letters that followed sharpened my curiosity regarding diabetes. Dr. Banting also sent me a copy of an article written with Charles Best on the internal secretion of the pancreas, which was to be published in the *Journal of Laboratory and Clinical Medicine*. I was fascinated. A sentence in one of his letters would change my life. He more or less said: "we have a lot of work and will soon need to expand our team."

I sent a telegram to Dr. Banting and asked if I could be of any help. Anyway, I still had to do a residency to complete my medical studies.

~ *PART TWO* ~

~ *CHAPTER 10* ~

So that was that, I was leaving. I made the decision on the spot, thinking of nothing else. My medal would no doubt help me to get working papers for Canada. It was also important to have a transit visa for the United States. The easiest way to go to Toronto was to take the boat to San Francisco, and then the train. I had to inform my family. As I expected, my parents had no trouble understanding my determination. But next I had to talk to Mac and Florence.

With Mac, it was easy. He still had a few months before graduation. And afterwards, he was thinking about finding a lab where he could work on epidemics.

With Florence, it would be more difficult. How could I tell her that I was going so far away? How would she react? Would she wait for me? The prospect of my departure sharpened my desire for her.

In early 1922, it was hot in Melbourne, even hotter than usual. We made love, at length, passionately, despite the sweltering heat. We swam in the pool, and then started again, without saying a word. I lacked the energy or the courage needed to tell her I was going away for several months. I was waiting for the right moment. In fact it was she who spoke first at the most exquisite moment – after lovemaking.

"Paul, there's something I have to tell you. I've found a very interesting residency in a hospital in Brisbane. We're going to have to separate for a while. I hope you won't hold it against me? You understand, don't you?"

"Of course. Besides, everyone recommended we find placements at the end of medical school. It's rewarding to see other cities and ways of life, new people... cold weather..."

"What are you talking about, Paul? It's never cold in Brisbane."

"Sorry, I don't know what I'm saying."

"What's wrong? You're upset. Is it what I just said?"

"Yes... no, a bit, but that's life. I'll miss you."

"I'll miss you too."

And we made love again with even more enthusiasm in the humid heat of the Australian summer.

It was only later that I told her I was leaving too. I had got word from Toronto. Dr. Banting had found me a room on the University campus. Everything was ready for the big trip. I was going to take the boat for the first time since the war, with travel companions who would not be crippled soldiers. I was going to cross the Pacific this time. Soon I would have been around the world.

San Francisco Bay was beautiful with its backdrop of bare mountains and radiant sun. Nobody was waiting for me. I was free to explore the city and America. Crowded sidewalks, streets shared by convertible motorcars, horse carts and trams. The cable cars were a real spectacle on the steep streets. From the cable car that was taking me from the port towards the centre of town I watched wide-eyed. I felt like a child again, enthralled by all the city noise and the movement and the tram drivers who operated the large golden lever with such fervour. The elegant women wore long black dresses and big hats, each fancier than the one before, for protection from the sun. The men were almost all dressed the same way, black frock coats, hats and ties. Here and there, amidst the beauty, were ruined houses, traces of the terrible earthquake that had ravaged the city in 1906. I couldn't stay in the city long, alas. I travelled by cable car directly to the station and a Chicago-bound train. Sitting on the wooden seat, I fell asleep, exhausted.

I slept for hours. No one woke me. I had enough food in my luggage to last me to Chicago. We arrived. There was no time for me to walk around there, either. I couldn't wait to get to Toronto. I still had a little more than one day of travel ahead of me. The cold weather, which I had never experienced, began to overwhelm me. I had forgotten it was winter there. Soon we'd see snow in the vastness we were travelling across. Industrial cities, full of tall chimneys belching black smoke. At the border crossing, the train stopped but no one came to check my papers. Lake Ontario. A body of water, or rather of ice, bleached by snow, a kind of sea whose opposite shore we could not see. Finally, Union Station, Toronto. I got off the train. The air was cold as ice, and the sky was grey. Everything was dark and gloomy. *What am I doing here?* I asked myself, shivering and chilled to the bone. But the thought of exciting new research helped me to overcome my disappointment.

The university proved easy to find, as people had said it would be. You walked up University Avenue and there it was.

The buildings eerily resembled those of the University of Melbourne, maybe a little more grey. British style. Green spaces between the buildings.

"Do you know where I can find Dr. Banting? Frederick Banting?"

Obviously nobody knew him. But when I asked the location of Professor McLeod's laboratory, I was immediately given all the details. I had to turn back, the pharmacology department being located in the Old Medical Building. Cold walls, and outside, large corridors without heating. A central staircase. A laboratory behind glass doors.

"Hello, where can I find Dr. Banting's laboratory?"

"Last door on the right," some unfriendly person replied.

Outside the door, on which nothing was written, I took a deep breath. I'd made that endless journey to find myself in front of a closed door. Had he changed? Was he waiting for me? Would I find a big sparkling laboratory, equipped with the most modern equipment? Should I knock... or leave?

~ *CHAPTER 11* ~

I knocked at the door. Only in dreams are things ever perfect. The laboratory was not at all what I had imagined. Far from it! Just a little square room, cramped and rundown. In the middle, a lab bench with a wooden shelf on top. The floor was wood too. As for the equipment... it was non-existent. Even classrooms in Melbourne were better equipped. There was a mingled smell of cigarette smoke, wet dog and urine. But there were no animals in sight when I entered. I knocked several times and getting no answer, opened the door and glanced around. There was nobody in. Not a sound. Yellowed lab dishes and spatulas were strewn all over the bench.

I sat waiting on a broken chair for nearly two hours before a man of about my age opened the door.

"Ah, a visitor. A visitor who looks somewhat the worse for wear. Tired, I would guess."

"A little. I'm Paul Dormont from Melbourne. And you're Charles Best, I would guess."

"Don't stand on ceremony. Call me Charley, everyone else does. Pleased to meet you. Fred said you were arriving, but we didn't know when. Would you like something to drink? I can boil water on the Bunsen burner for tea. We're short of coffee."

"A cup of tea then, but I don't want to bother you. Are the labs always this cold?"

"Mm, yes... especially this one. The heating has trouble getting all the way to the end of the hall."

"And how is Dr. Banting?"

"Fred, call him Fred, it'll annoy him if you don't. He's fine. Actually, he's tired. He never stops working."

"Where? This laboratory has no equipment!"

"Most of our experiments are done on animals in a little room down the hall. That's where he is. He'll be here any minute."

Fred's arrival was just as I had imagined. Warm. He welcomed me with open arms, obviously happy to see me, and bombarded me with questions about myself, my health, and my life in general.

"Charley, it's time for lunch. Let's give our new assistant a proper welcome."

We went to a restaurant near the university. The conversation immediately turned to science. Fred and Charley were full of enthusiasm, eager to talk about their scientific adventures. They told me everything, from the very beginning.

"As I wrote you, Paul, my experience as a GP in London was not a great success. But two years ago, I got the chance to teach physiology to medical students for a few hours a week. Two dollars an hour... starvation wages. One day, I had to give a class on the metabolism of carbohydrates. As an orthopaedic surgeon, you can imagine that I knew nothing about the subject. I read Barron's article, the one I told you about. Did you manage to read it?"

"Yes, otherwise I wouldn't be here."

"So you agree with his theory, an internal pancreatic

secretion with special cells that can prevent glycosuria? We're beginning to find solid evidence that the theory is true, as you saw in our first article with Charley. But here, in this building, there are still doubters. Especially the director. He is to be called Professor McLeod. Very unfriendly... his secretary too. He stuck us all the way back here, away from everybody, probably to avoid contagion. He doesn't like the doctors like me who have a passion for research because, according to him, that's not what doctors are supposed to do. That is why I brought Charley along. He's a real scientist."

"Don't you believe it!" protested Charley. "I'm a student and I haven't even finished my exams in physiology and biochemistry. And I only got here last year in May."

"McLeod doesn't see why I should succeed where famous scientists have run into brick walls," said Fred. "Like Paulesco, a Romanian who wrote only in French in *les Comptes Rendus des séances de la Société de Biologie*. Incidentally, Paul, you'll help me understand what Paulesco says. He claims to have successfully completed animal experiments with pancreatic extracts. I don't believe his results. The sugar levels he measured aren't compatible with ours. There are still a lot of problems to be solved, but in the year I've been here we've made progress, thanks to Charley."

"You should eat, Fred, your meat will be cold," said Charley.

I knew already that people who were passionate about something could forget everything else, even eating and sleeping. John Monash, for example. You only had to get him started on his favourite subject, the war, and nothing could stop him. It was the same with Fred, who kept on talking without even looking at his plate.

"We lost a lot of time because we had to wait weeks, just as Barron said, for the acinar cells of the pancreas to degenerate after duct ligation. Unfortunately, the extraction of pancreatic substance didn't have many beneficial effects on diabetic dogs. Last summer, Professor McLeod, back from vacation in Scotland, criticised our work, and no doubt he was partially right. We're not chemists, and the extraction of isletin, as we call it, is far from perfect."

"But you've got no equipment in your lab!"

"You're right, Paul, but a new and bigger lab is ready for us... and we were just waiting for your arrival to move into it. Professor McLeod has even offered to pay you, though not much. I think he's starting to understand that our work has a chance of succeeding. When, I don't know now; but I know we will."

I was tired and could no longer concentrate on what Fred was saying.

"It's time I took you to your lodgings. It's no palace, but it's better than the trenches."

I managed a faint smile.

I slept like a log for over twenty hours, as if the Earth had stopped turning. I took a day to get settled and buy food for the next little while. But I was eager to get started.

First, a week of operating on animals with Fred. When I started, my fingers were always frozen, but I got used to it quickly. Operating was a delicate affair, but not impossible. The most important thing was to monitor the effects of the anaesthesia to avoid losing the animals. My presence allowed Charley to devote more time to sugar in the blood and urine.

"Hello, gentlemen, how are you today?" To all appearances, Professor McLeod was in fine fettle.

"You must be the young Australian doctor Fred told me about. Welcome. What did you learn there? Anatomy, tropical medicine, anthropology, all those subjects of little interest to us?"

"No, sir, I learned neurology and basic sciences like physiology and biochemistry."

"In that case you interest me, young man."

At that moment there was a knock at the door, and an elegant man of Fred's age entered the laboratory.

"Allow me to introduce Dr. Collip, Bert Collip, our brilliant biochemist, who is with us on sabbatical. He's from the University of Alberta. It's even colder there than here, I'm told! Bert helps us purify the pancreatic substance. He's working to perfect methods of extraction and purification, and making good progress. Fred and Charley make an efficient couple, but Bert is overloaded with work that is critical to the project's success. What would you say if I asked you to work with him?"

I was not going to oppose the boss's decision. And that is how I became a biochemist.

~ *CHAPTER 12* ~

James Collip, whom everyone called Bert, had to return to Alberta for several days, so I did my operations with Fred. During the long hours we spent in the animal house, Fred summarised the results from the dogs he had already operated on. He gesticulated while speaking.

"All the dogs must have a ligation of the pancreatic duct so that we can obtain diabetes mellitus after a few weeks. The pancreas atrophies and degenerates. Then we remove the atrophied organ and administer pancreatic extracts to the animal. These contain the internal secretion from the acini. Day after day we monitor the evolution and survival. Our first dog was number 385. Why? Don't ask me, I've forgotten. That was in May. Unfortunately, due to infection and to the extreme heat that summer of '21, we lost all our animals. Still, Charley managed to prepare extracts and we injected our first dog in late July. That time they all died too. We got the first results on August 8. I remember that day. We were so happy to have positive results that we danced in the lab and drank a little too much, I admit. Our pancreatic extract produced a reduction of sugar levels in the blood and an improvement in the animal's clinical condition. The extract would normally keep at least four days, but the heat destroyed it. Only the pancreatic juice was active. That of the other organs was ineffective. Charley will probably tell you about Marjorie, number 33, our favourite bitch. There's a photo of her on the wall, taken in January. Thanks to Marjorie, we decided to move on to the clinic. We started injecting patients with our extracts last month. I think it was a little premature, Paul. We observed a slight decrease in blood sugar, but the main problem was infection."

"Is that why Bert is trying to purify the extract?"

"Charley, too," Fred replied drily.

There seemed to be tension between them.

Fred sometimes flew into rages, often directed against himself, when things did not turn out the way he wanted. At those times, it was better to hold one's tongue.

Fortunately Charley was there to lighten the mood. He spent a great deal of time in the lab, but still tried to escape from time to time to see his friends and Margaret, his fiancée.

"I'm going to the pub with friends tonight. It's my birthday. Paul, would you like to come? The dogs are sleeping, they don't need you."

Charley had a lot of friends. True, he had done his entire education in Toronto. He liked to celebrate, have fun, enjoy every moment of life.

In the place where we spent the evening, the smoke was unbearable. It was hard to talk over the music, and the conversations were too loud. I only remember the name of one of his friends. Clark, Clark Noble, who sometimes worked in the laboratory. Charley stayed very close to Margaret all evening. They formed an ideal couple, like in the movies.

"So, do you like the atmosphere here? No air? You know,

alcohol is precious here; it helps us through the long winter months. Don't worry, the girls will arrive soon. It takes them a while to get ready."

The end of the evening was more pleasant. I got used to the atmosphere and then a dozen girls came to join us, all with boyish hairstyles and wearing fringed dresses, wondering whom the new face belonged to. An Australian. Perhaps they were disappointed that I wasn't an Aborigine! An Aborigine who would dance with them: the Charleston, foxtrot, or tap dance to the frenzied rhythms of Ray Miller. You had to be careful not to get your eye poked out by the feathers in the fashionable hats, or twisted in a voluminous boa, or long necklaces of fake pearls around their necks that whirled in the air.

The return to the lab was difficult, especially as a very angry Fred roundly scolded us.

"You've got off to a bad start, Paul. I suppose it was Charley that dragged you into debauchery? You left the lab in a terrible mess. The solutions dried up on the bench. You have to discard them after they've been used, and wash everything. If you want to avoid contamination, you're not to leave anything lying around. It's difficult enough as it is to get the extracts right, and in a mess like this, there's no point in even trying. If this continues, I'll show you the door. Charley, if you're no more interested in research, I can easily replace you with your pal Clark Noble."

We could not or did not want to answer. It would have been hard to tell him that it was Charley's birthday. Fred was so angry that he wasn't listening. But reprimands always serve a purpose. They separate people but also draw them closer.

We resumed our work with even greater zeal. This episode

had brought me closer to Charley. Being scolded together had created a tie between the two of us.

"Tell me, Charley, Fred's reactions can't make his relations with Professor McLeod any easier?"

"To say the least!"

"It looks as if they hate each other. But they have everything they need to succeed. Fred told me a lot about your work and the results you've had. Amazing, isn't it?"

"Did Fred tell you everything? Did he talk about his situation, and the symposium he went to with Professor McLeod in New Haven, Connecticut?"

"No."

"Listen to this. I think it all began when Fred asked Professor McLeod, who was just back from vacation in Scotland, for a larger workspace, plus some help with the animals, and refurbishing of the operating room floor. I was there. McLeod hesitated. He criticised our results, based on too few animals, according to him. And we had gone over our quota. I was there and it went badly."

"And why re-do the operating room if we are moving to a new location?"

Fred had given Professor McLeod an ultimatum that verged on blackmail:

"If you don't give me what I ask for in two days, I'm leaving," he said. "I'll quit, despite all the sacrifices I've made to do this research."

"And what will you do?" McLeod replied.

"I'll go sell myself elsewhere. I'll sell my ideas. To the Mayo Clinic, for example."

"Stuff and nonsense," McLeod had said. "Even the Rockefeller Institute has terminated research on the subject."

"That's not true; the Institute continues to do diabetes

research, although the clinical results are disappointing, you know it as well as I do. It is in our interest to find a common ground. If you refuse, I'll tell the University of Toronto."

"Mr. Banting, I am the University of Toronto."

"I thought they were going to fight," Charley continued. "After a long silence, McLeod spoke again: "Very well. I'll try to meet your expectations. But this is really the last time."

As we walked, I told Charley that I had never seen anyone speak that way to the professor.

"And that's not all. A few months ago in New Haven, Professor McLeod asked Fred to present our first results, to the *American Society of Physiology*, of which he is President. I must admit Fred wasn't very good. He wasn't a good enough speaker to present our results to their full advantage. He probably had the jitters. He was afraid our colleagues might reject his hypothesis, which he is so keen on. I was embarrassed for him. Then Professor McLeod took the floor to answer questions. Fred was none too pleased. He felt offended. But basically, Professor McLeod was right to speak up. He was trying to save our work. Still, Fred hasn't forgiven him. Since then, he's been convinced that McLeod wants to reap the benefits of our discoveries. Because he's the boss and he is known in the field, Fred thinks he'll be the one to gain recognition from our colleagues."

"That's absurd. It's like children squabbling at kindergarten."

"A little, but researchers are big kids... like us."

"Charley, I have to tell you, Professor McLeod's decision to make me work with Bert bothers me. With Fred I get the feeling that if you're not with him, you're his enemy."

"I don't believe that. You have nothing to do with it, and dealings with Bert are not as tense, though he is wary of him.

Bert brings a lot to the team with his knowledge of chemistry. We can only progress if it helps us get an even purer product without toxic effects."

"Oh, because there have been toxic effects?"

"First of all, we don't yet have a substance that definitely comes from the internal secretion of the pancreas only. When we inject a substance that has not been purified, toxic effects are sometimes observed."

"But then, how can we hope to cure a great number of people?"

"We're almost there, Paul. Fred must have told you that with the help of the clinical medicine department, we tried injections on a young man. He wanted the first preparation to be his, that is, ours. Unfortunately it wasn't very effective. But Bert's preparation was more active. The young man responded extremely well and his blood sugar has dropped significantly. Other patients have begun treatment, among them a young girl, who weighed only fifty pounds and couldn't walk when she was admitted to hospital a few weeks ago. Fred is always on guard, but he understands that he won't succeed on his own. The Dean of the Faculty of Pharmacology, Professor Henderson, got a teaching job for him, and Professor McLeod helped with his salary. I also got a small wage. Since then, Fred has been doing better. I am sure that he hasn't told you, but he lived frugally in a one-room apartment, like a student, and often skipped meals. He regretted not being able to get me a salary. What can you do, research is not an ideal job for keeping body and soul together!"

~ *CHAPTER 13* ~

I worked with Bert Collip in another building, the pathology unit of the Toronto General Hospital. Was that what Professor McLeod had wanted? Maybe. In any case, our biochemistry laboratory was well equipped. Bert was a charming man, caring and sensitive. He was only thirty. He had already taught for two years in Alberta and written over twenty publications. He was a husband and a father. In one week, working beside him, I learned all the necessary techniques for purifying pancreatic extracts. Canine pancreatic ligation was no longer a requirement. And Fred and Charley had obtained very convincing results reducing sugar levels in the blood using pancreatic extracts from foetal calves obtained at the slaughterhouse, and even more interesting results with sheep and adult pig pancreas. Therefore, there was no need for lengthy operations. Bert had also developed a more sensitive technique for sugar dosage.

I reread the article by Fred and Charley on the internal secretion of the pancreas just published in the February issue of the prestigious *Journal of Laboratory and Clinical Medicine*. At first glance, I did not notice that Professor McLeod had not signed it. Then I understood. They must have still been bickering about it. However, Bert told me that Professor McLeod had deliberately declined to co-sign this excellent article because the work was entirely that of Fred and Charley. But I had noticed errors in the figures and a misinterpretation in the discussion of the results previously published by Nicolas Paulesco in French. But I wanted to avoid another angry outburst from Fred.

"Paul, be careful. We have to meticulously examine the tissue from the slaughterhouse. You know what a pancreas looks like?" said Bert.

"What do you take me for? I'm not a beginner. I'm an MD, ain't I? Why are you asking such a stupid question?"

"Because when I got here in December with my sabbatical grant from the Rockefeller Foundation, I took another look at the alcoholic extracts made by Fred and Charley. I didn't get the same results."

"Do you think they cheated?"

"No, it's funnier than that. The fellow from the animal house brought extracts from thymus or thyroid glands instead of the pancreas. Naturally, it never decreased the blood sugar."

"They're just pulling your leg, right?"

"A little... even a lot." And Bert burst out laughing, one of those infectious laughs.

"And now you test your thymus on rabbits!" I was overcome with uncontrollable laughter.

Bert had noticed that good pancreatic extracts of different species could decrease even the basal plasma glucose level of normal rabbits. This observation was a great advance and allowed us to test new extracts quickly.

"Paul, I've watched how Charley prepares his extracts. It's never good to evaporate an alcohol solution completely. It is better to reduce it, keep a small fraction of liquid that can then be filtered. That way we can obtain a liquid solution on the one hand and a solid residue on the other. Can you try?"

The test on diabetic dogs was conclusive. Not only had sugar dropped, but the ketone bodies too. The "mysterious thing," as Bert called it, could cure diabetes. Yet we had to remain cautious. In fact, every time we injected a rabbit, we perceived he was hungry and devoured everything he could find. This urge to eat was correlated with a decrease of sugar in the blood. Some even had seizures and a sort of coma, and died quickly.

"Do you think, Paul, that alcoholic extracts may be toxic?"

"Maybe, but I think it's more likely to be a hypoglycaemic shock. I've seen that before. Give our injected rabbits some sugar and we'll see."

The answer was clear: the animals recovered. So it was really the drop in sugar caused by the pancreatic extract that produced the coma. Fred had changed the name of 'isletin' to 'insulin'. We decided to call our phenomenon 'insulin shock'.

I had lunch at noon with Charley and his friends at the university restaurant. Bert had his meals with Professor McLeod in the Hart House dining room, reserved for teachers. Fred went there often. During one of these lunches, Professor McLeod told Bert that George Clowes, director of research at Eli Lilly and Co, had phoned him. He wanted to work with our laboratory to prepare commercial extracts for use in humans.

"You, Bert, will be in charge of the relations with Clowes and Eli Lilly for purification. As a biochemist, you're the most knowledgeable on the subject."

"But Fred and Charley won't agree."

"I'll arrange for them to deal with the physiological part."

"Good luck."

As could be expected, Fred's reaction was fierce.

"In that case, as a doctor, I'll do the first injections on patients," said Fred.

"You have to discuss that with Professor Duncan Graham, who is head of the clinical unit," McLeod answered drily, pulling on the pipe that was still in his mouth.

"I'm on my way."

"Conspiracy," was the word that Fred blurted. "Conspiracy! Those bastards don't even want me to treat the sick people. Graham refused on the grounds that I didn't have the qualifications or accreditation for this, being a surgeon, 'not a practitioner'!"

Furious, he entered Professor McLeod's office.

"What's the plot against me now? Is it the Scottish Mafia? Is it you who said to your friend Graham that I'm unable to administer extracts to patients?"

"No, Graham said he couldn't give his consent."

"Do something to keep this from going too far."

"I promise that we will start by testing your preparation, at least, the purest you can get, with Charley. I rely on your ability to provide the best extract, if possible, previously tested on your experimental dog."

Charley told me all this over lunch. I was not even in Toronto at the time. These heated exchanges had taken place in December and February, just before my arrival at the laboratory. I had never imagined that research could generate so much hatred.

~ *CHAPTER 14* ~

Leonard Thompson had been admitted to Dr. Walter Campbell's diabetes clinic, Toronto General Hospital, in early December 1921. He was fourteen years old and suffered from advanced diabetes. The boy was emaciated, his bones visible under his skin that was as thin as cigarette paper. He weighed only sixty-five pounds after following the absurd diet inflicted on diabetes patients, based on the precepts developed by Allen in the United States.

The young Leonard had received an injection of beef pancreas extract that had been previously tested. His sugar level had dropped from 0440 to 0320 in the blood and urine, but there was no improvement in the ketones. They had to face facts: the result was disappointing.

Leonard was dying. Something had to be done. The decision was made to try Bert's extracts. Bert knew the reactions of Fred and Charley were going to be unpleasant. Yet we had reached an agreement; we prepared the extracts, and Fred and Charley conducted the experiments. It was doctors like Graham and probably premature testing on humans that led us to modify our agreement. We could not go back. We had to help Leonard.

The local press got involved. A reporter from the *Toronto*

Star, tipped off by heaven-knows-who, wanted the scoop. He came to interview Professor McLeod, who could not say anything besides "we are still working on a cure for this terrible disease". Poor Leonard was perhaps too ill to benefit from treatment.

Naturally the 'we' of the interview infuriated Fred and Charley. But at least the journalist, at the request of Professor McLeod, agreed not to talk about the poor results.

Bert asked me not to leave the laboratory until we came up with extracts that were sufficiently pure. He himself spent his life at the lab bench, forgetting to eat and drink. We constantly modified our preparations, so it was impossible to know which was the best recipe. We had to distil, filter, desalinate, and dissolve the preparation in alcohol. No time to take notes.

"Bert, did you see that when you add alcohol to over 90%, the 'mysterious thing' speeds up?"

"Fantastic. That way we can catch it." We tested the product on our rabbits. It worked. We could return to Leonard.

Late that night, Bert and I went to Fred and Charley's lab. We wanted to tell them that we could get an alcohol form of the insulin that lowered sugar in the blood and urine.

"Congratulations on your purely technical feat of little interest," Fred replied curtly.

"What do you mean little interest? You know, Fred, that to treat humans we need a substance whose synthesis we're sure to master and that we can then purify and analyse."

"And how did you do it?"

"I can't tell you."

"Why not? We work well together, don't we?"

"Yes, but you hurt my feelings, Fred, and I think it's time for us to sign a real contract that commits us for the future."

I sensed that Fred was fuming inside.

"So you're betraying us too?"

I was afraid that Fred would get to his feet and knock Bert down. Fortunately Charley intervened.

"Let's everyone calm down. All this confrontation gets us nowhere. We are all at fault in this affair. The agreement has to reflect the work each of us has done, so if one day we find a cure for diabetes, our colleagues will recognise our respective contributions."

It took the intervention of several people from the university for us to reach an agreement. It looked more like conciliation before a divorce judge than a cordial negotiation. The cooperation agreement between the four scientists and Connaught Anti-Toxin Laboratories, a local laboratory called upon to prepare larger quantities of extracts, stated that researchers at the University of Toronto should continue working together to obtain a pancreas extract that could be patented for use in humans, and that nothing could be decided or changed in this agreement without a meeting attended by all the participants named.

We were all exhausted, even I, who had no interest in the agreement. I no longer knew if I could still talk to Fred and Charley. I wondered if I shouldn't simply leave the research world, which I had never imagined as hostile. So even intelligent people could come to hate each other!

These episodes had increased the tobacco consumption in the lab and also that of alcohol. One depressing evening, Charley found Fred dead drunk in his room, probably a result of too much emotional pressure. Fred had broken up with his fiancée, Edith Roach.

It was probably the children and the emaciated teenagers lying in their beds at the diabetes clinic that saved the laboratory. We understood, thanks to the intervention of people outside the laboratory, like Henderson, Hunter, Starr and Fitzgerald, that it was time to end the internal struggles that were only delaying the research. The process developed by Bert seemed to work. Leonard had received new injections of the extract prepared by Fred and Charley according to the new method. Ketonuria disappeared, and sugar levels went from .0520 to .0120. Furthermore, Marjorie the dog was still alive after the removal of her pancreas, thus demonstrating that the extract was not toxic in the long term.

We also had to think about writing our papers without being overtaken. It wasn't a simple matter. Fred and Charley just wanted to write articles about their first results, from the dog with the pancreatic duct ligation. McLeod wanted to write a report on the meeting in New Haven, and Bert about data on methods of purifying pancreatic extracts and improvement of the Shaffer-Hartman technique to measure sugar in blood and urine.

The *Toronto Star* had published an article on us, including an interview with Fred. However, the article, though well written, failed to pique the readers' interest.

~ *CHAPTER 15* ~

Insulin. The choice of this word, from a Latin root meaning 'little island', instead of 'isletin', was not a problem. But later we learned that the word 'insulin' had already been proposed by Schafer in 1916 to describe the internal secretion of the pancreas. Schafer in turn was unaware that Meyer before him had made the same suggestion in 1909.

If Fred was struggling to get back to work, it was probably because he felt that something was eluding him. He could not treat patients himself. He had not mastered the techniques required to isolate insulin, and the university was more interested in the lucrative side of things. George Clowes, director of research at Eli Lilly, an Indianapolis research group, had attended the New Haven colloquium and remained informed about our team's progress. Fred and Professor McLeod had rejected Clowes's first invitation to work with him. They felt, rightly, that the work on the purification of pancreatic extracts was not sufficiently advanced. But Clowes had understood the importance of such research in Toronto. He insisted that the two laboratories collaborate. The university and Professor McLeod saw this as financial assistance, Bert as a way to file a patent. Charley was not really against it, but

Fred, despite past financial struggles, did not want us to take out a patent on insulin.

"Insulin can't be patented. It has to be accessible to all for the welfare of humanity. If you want to patent it, count me out. I'll give it to you for a symbolic dollar."

It was already May. The snow had finally melted. When I think of those four winter months in Toronto, the tension in the lab, and the ache inside of me which made me want to go home, I reflect that, in spite of it all, I was lucky to have been there, be part of this adventure, and to mingle with the key protagonists of an extraordinary discovery. I explained all this in the first long letter that I sent to my parents. Charley didn't go out anymore either, except with Margaret. There had been no further nights on the town since his birthday. Maybe that would change when the weather warmed up.

I was preparing to leave for the congress of the *Association of American Physicians* in Washington. Following the agreement, for once, no one objected to Professor McLeod making the presentation himself. All the major diabetologists were there: Allen, Solis-Cohen, Woodyatt, Joslin. Professor McLeod's presentation was scheduled for lunchtime. It began in a cathedral-like silence.

"For over two years, our group in Toronto has worked very hard to develop a treatment for diabetes. That is, a physiological treatment of this disease. The idea germinated in the mind of Dr. Frederick Banting, whom some of you heard last year in New Haven. As it is often the case in research, we have had our ups and downs."

Professor McLeod began to show pictures, curves, and the positive but also negative results we had obtained.

"You can see that finding the right path requires time and determination. Tact and luck too. Charles Best, a student in his fourth year of Science at the University of Toronto, has played a role in achieving these results. He oversaw the dosages while Dr. Banting operated on the animals and prepared the pancreatic extracts. Then came Dr. James Bertram Collip, who is here today and whom few of you know, as he is mainly a biochemist and a professor at the University of Alberta. Thanks to his special skills, we were able to improve our extraction procedures for the internal substance of the pancreas, a substance we called 'insulin'. As you know, with the help of Professor Walter Campbell of the Toronto General Hospital, to date we have treated two patients with diabetes whose results I will now present."

Whispers could be heard all over the room, then exclamations of surprise at the test results: a dramatic fall in blood sugar and urine ketones. There were pictures of Leonard and Dr. Joe Gilchrist, a diabetic classmate of Fred's. The audience stood up, one after the other, applauding wildly.

No one even heard Professor McLeod's last words:

"We have discovered insulin."

I was lucky to be there. Bert had funded my trip to Washington. Unfortunately, Fred and Charley were not present to witness their triumph. They had excused themselves at the last moment due to the high cost of travel...

On our return to Toronto, the cooperation agreement between our laboratory and Eli Lilly was ready. The company would not interfere with research, but would produce insulin on a large scale for commercial purposes. Charley and Bert went to Indianapolis to explain to the chemists how to prepare the extracts.

As I passed Fred's lab, I caught sight of him at his desk.

"Fred, instead of sitting there alone, come to lunch with me. Everyone else has left for the United States and it's just the two of us, other than Professor McLeod."

"Very well, but you must promise not to talk about insulin."

And of course, after a bit of small talk, memories of the Battle of the Somme, and some thoughts on painting, which was Fred's other passion, he began talking about insulin.

"I'm really not cut out for research. Even if it hadn't worked out, I should have kept my office and continued seeing patients. Operating is what I love to do. Today my ideas, my discoveries are known to the general public. I'm not even sure we'll be able to treat diabetics in the long term. People are excited about this discovery, but we don't even know if our product is pure, or whether, over time, it is likely to induce toxic effects. It makes me sick. Now that I think of it, a new war would give us something else to think about."

"You're crazy, Fred. How can you talk like that when you were at such a loss to describe the horror of trench warfare? Do you realise what you're saying? Wake up! Look at reality. You may have made the greatest medical discovery of all time! Isn't saving people what Hippocrates urged us to do? Stop being so fussy. Eli Lilly will contribute a lot of money to our research. Maybe we'll get new labs with the latest equipment. We'll be the envy of our colleagues all over the world. How can you sit there moping when the whole medical community stood and applauded you in Washington? I was there, I saw it all!"

"Applauding McLeod, you mean."

"Don't be a fool. He sang your praises and ours too. Professor McLeod is probably not as detestable as you think. And he is the head of the lab. He defends his lab and the discoveries made there. That's how things should be. It's the same with some military leaders we have known. Some got more illustrious medals than yours or mine... and yet what a lot of strategic errors they made! And if certain people, like John Monash, hadn't got them out of the hole, where would we be now?"

"Here we go again with Monash!"

"Yes, because, you see, he was dismissed after his return to Australia. People were worried he might replace some utterly incompetent politicians. But they hadn't understood that what was most important for Monash wasn't politics but his men, the 'diggers' and his passion for engineering."

"You're right. Let me start again. My friend Henderson, professor of pharmacology, said the same thing as you. Not about Monash, of course."

"Fred? You're a military doctor, aren't you?"

"Yes, why?"

"It probably hasn't occurred to you, but if you asked to work in a military hospital in Toronto, you might be able to get patients without going through Campbell. Think about it."

~ *CHAPTER 16* ~

Under pressure from the university, Bert and Charley had drafted an application for a Canadian patent on biological extraction methods. In addition, Eli Lilly had understood that insulin could earn them a fortune.

But nothing turned out as planned. With Bert, we hadn't succeeded in making new insulin. We worked night and day, to no avail. Bert was worried:

"If this continues, we'll be running out of insulin."

Bad news soon came from the hospital.

"A girl died this morning. We didn't have enough insulin to treat her."

It quickly appeared to us that temperature played an important role. Charley had already observed that too high a temperature destroys insulin. The device we used for evaporating the alcohol must have malfunctioned. It produced too much heat. We had to go back to the old method of evaporation with hot air, developed by Charley. The use of acetone instead of alcohol allowed for evaporation at a lower temperature. And then the miracle happened: by adding a slight acidification, as suggested by Professor McLeod, we had insulin again. But Bert did not like this type of preparation; it was too dangerous, considering how many fire hazards there were in the laboratory.

Fred's verve had returned. My risky idea had succeeded. Fred had got work at the military hospital on Christie Street, and we divided the production of insulin between the lab and the hospitals. He was back in his chosen field, medicine. Every day he received letters from colleagues asking him for insulin. Although Eli Lilly had the exclusive rights of production, the method had been registered and could now be duplicated in any laboratory.

Bert's sabbatical period was coming to an end. He was going back to Alberta. What could I possibly work on alone?

"Fred, do you know that Bert is leaving us to go back to Alberta? What will I do? My residency is over soon."

"Surely you don't think I'm going to drop you, Paul, just because you worked for 'the enemy'? What do you want to do? Stay, or go back to Melbourne? You need a vacation like the rest of us, and you haven't seen your folks for a long time. You certainly have lots to tell them. And a word in passing: if you do go and want to come back... you will always be welcome."

I was tempted to go back to Melbourne. Recharge my batteries. However, the best time in Toronto is the summer, when it's hot. You can swim in the lake, rent a paddle-boat, and sit on the beach with some of the most beautiful girls in the city.

"Fred is right," said Charley. "I'm going to take a little rest too. Otherwise I'm afraid Margaret will get tired of waiting and leave me. I don't spend enough time with her. Never get engaged if you want to do research!"

Professor McLeod was going to spend the summer at the marine research station in St. Andrews, New Brunswick, to work on fish insulin.

So Fred was all on his own in Toronto. How would he cope with the rising demand for insulin, and the increasing number of patients who arrived each day? Connaught did not have enough insulin. To make matters worse, the laboratory extractor had broken down.

Fred spoke directly to the chairman of the university's board of governors.

"I need $10,000 right away in order to save lives."

"But the whole office is on vacation, Dr. Banting. I can't assume this responsibility alone."

"You realise what you're doing?"

"But the office only opens again in September."

"And meanwhile you just let people die? This is outrageous!"

Fred emerged furious, slamming the chairman's door behind him. He knew that wealthy Americans asked their doctors to do everything in their power to save their sick children. Fred knew one such American, in New York. Over the phone, the reply was immediate. What was the quickest way for money to be sent to the University of Toronto?

Fred went back to see the chairman.

"Mr. Chairman, I would like to know if your damn office would accept a cheque for US $10,000."

"I see no objection."

"In that case, I will immediately order a new extractor."

Fred phoned New York again.

"My dear colleague, if you ever need insulin, let me know. You're first on my list. Thank you for your help."

Eli Lilly also received urgent requests from major US

departments of diabetology. For the sake of the company's prestige, a special issue on the treatment of diabetes with insulin had to be published. In this issue, they would naturally be mentioned. And they needed Dr. Frederick Banting's scientific backing.

Just before I left for Melbourne, Fred told us about this request. The letter from Clowes stated: 'If you accept our invitation, it may consecrate you for the highest of all distinctions'.

~ *CHAPTER 17* ~

Charley wrote me in Melbourne to tell me about his vacation in Maine and to inform me that pig insulin, now manufactured by Eli Lilly and Connaught, was producing spectacular results. No news from Bert or Professor McLeod. Charley's letter also said that Fred was busy saving Elizabeth Hughes, the daughter of an American Secretary of State and member of the Supreme Court. It startled me to read the name. For a moment I thought it was the daughter of our Prime Minister, the man John Monash hated. I was relieved that Charley had said she was American.

Monash continued to be involved in many activities. I could see him and Lizette, only once during my short stay in Melbourne. He had the time to tell me that, thanks to him, every home in Melbourne would soon have electricity, and that he was about to become vice-chancellor of the university, a true homecoming. My father had reduced his own activities at the university, but my mother continued to work at the Women's Hospital in Melbourne, mainly in oncology.

Mac had found his calling. The following year, he would go to the Walter and Eliza Hall Institute at Melbourne University to do research on the reactions of agglutinin in typhoid fever.

As for Florence, no one had heard from her. My decision was made. I went back to Toronto.

The colours of autumn had arrived. I had been told this was the best season in Canada. The leaves were of every shade of the palette, ranging from green to flaming red. The reflection in the lake emphasised their vivid hues.

The atmosphere in the laboratory had become more serene. Everything worked. Fred had managed the summer's difficulties perfectly and, in return, received the smiles of patients on the road to recovery. Praise continued to pour in from around the world. But what was I going to do? Work in the clinic with Fred, maybe. But I didn't have a Canadian degree. Bert was gone, insulin production was now being done outside the lab, and Charley was responsible for overseeing Connaught's lab work. Professor McLeod, who was also back from vacation, asked me to see if fish extracts produced an effect on carbohydrate metabolism, blood glucose and ketone bodies. According to him, fish contained insulin. Not very exciting, but good enough for the time being.

Charley also asked me to assist the Connaught lab technicians. That was my second job, for the time being. And so I had time to devote to writing the residency report I needed to send to Melbourne.

I told myself that Professor McLeod's laboratory was a real Shakespearean drama, but one with a happy ending. And I hadn't seen everything!

One morning, I found a summons from Professor McLeod on my desk. It was not like him to have us all meet in his office.

"Next week, we'll be getting a visit from Dr. Henry Dale,

the director of the British Medical Research Council, MRC. The English have finally heard about the work being done here at the Institute."

He took care not to use the 'we'.

"I don't believe they appreciate the fact that Canadians or Australians—or even Scots—have surpassed them. They want to check for themselves at the MRC that our basic work is valid. Fred, are you willing to have them visit your clinic?"

"I don't think it'll be hard to get authorization from the military hospital."

And so Henry Dale and the biochemist Harold Dudley took a dignified tour of our facilities.

"How do you do research with so little equipment? How do you manage to get these kinds of results in such conditions? I must say we were sceptical before coming here, but the effects of insulin, if indeed it is insulin, are conclusive. I was impressed by what we were told by the girl, Elizabeth Hughes, who has returned to normal weight after six months with you. She spoke of insulin as 'awfully wonderful'."

As usual, Fred was not satisfied.

"You heard him, Paul – 'if indeed it is insulin'. The English are as smug as ever. You'll see, it'll take them months to make a decision, while thousands of British patients are dying from diabetes, like our 'diggers', as you called them, in the trenches."

Requests for insulin kept pouring in. From Scandinavia, a letter from Professor August Krogh, who had just received the Nobel Prize in Physiology or Medicine, and one from Professor Oskar Minkowski in Breslau, Germany, a renowned diabetologist. Other letters, which Fred did not want to read or could not understand for linguistic reasons, came from scientists who asked for reprints of his publications, of which he had few copies, or simply said that Fred's idea was nothing new.

That was true, even if nobody had gone as far as we had in Toronto. Minkowski and Zuelzer in Germany, Keiner and Barron, of course, from the United States, Murlin from England, Paulesco from Romania, all had to stop their promising experiments on pancreatic extracts because of war or lack of financial means.

I could read the articles in French, unlike Fred, who had probably made errors of judgement through lack of understanding of some of Paulesco's articles. I learned that during a recent meeting of the prestigious *Société de Biologie* in Paris, an endocrinologist named Eugene Gley had opened a sealed letter he had filed in 1905, relating to his work on pancreatic extracts and showing they could reduce sugar levels in a diabetic dog. But he still acknowledged that he had no claim to being the father of insulin.

It must be said that research is an evolution of ideas, of concepts that emerge all at the same time because of technical progress. Fred had always said that had he not read Barron, he would never have drawn up his hypothesis. Fred had never doubted. And yet there are no certainties in science, so researchers always live in doubt. That may have been why Fred was not a genuine researcher... though a wonderful doctor.

~ *CHAPTER 18* ~

We had no news of Bert. But through articles in major periodicals, such as the *Journal of Biological Chemistry*, and *Nature*, we learned he was looking for insulin in yeast and plants. That was what Charley was doing, too, at the Connaught laboratories.

The world media reprinted the articles and interviews that appeared on each other's pages. Some were sceptical, like the English, of course, who were themselves unable to synthesise insulin correctly; others spoke of disputes over patents; still others related the successes but also the failures of insulin. It required great strength of character, like that of Fred, Charley or Professor McLeod, to avoid becoming emotional and wrangling with the press.

Once again, it was the British who put the match to the powder keg. Professor William Bayliss of University College, London, had just published an article in the *Times* chronicling the history of the discovery of insulin, attributing it to his friend Professor McLeod, aided by his assistant, Frederick Banting.

Again, Fred lashed out at McLeod, who had nothing to do with the article. McLeod had to reply via the *Toronto Star* that the Bayliss article contained errors, but his reply did not really call attention to the fact that Banting and Best were to be given credit for the discovery of insulin.

And so the old arguments surfaced again, all because of a newspaper article. "Bayliss would have done better to stay in his lab with his hormones instead of writing nonsense," Fred grumbled.

The University of Toronto Board of Governors was losing patience with these internal battles that gave a bad image of research in their institution. As a headmaster would have done with unruly students, the Board and its chairman summoned the warring parties to their office.

"Gentlemen, your behaviour is unacceptable. It's time to pull yourselves together. Our university can no longer tolerate actions that harm our reputation, while your discoveries are winning acclaim all over the world. I'm giving each of you a week to describe, in writing, your interpretation of the discovery of insulin and your personal involvement with it. I'll leave Professor Collip in his distant land of Alberta."

Alas, though the story was the same, each related it in his own way.

Professor McLeod emphasised the help given to Fred and Charley and his critical viewpoint in the beginning, when it was necessary to choose which direction to take. He described in detail the events of the New Haven conference and how he had been obliged to defend the group's interests. He emphasised his refusal to put his name on Banting and Best's first article, published the year before in the *Journal of Laboratory and Clinical Medicine*; he wanted them to have the 'scoop' on their discovery, despite the custom of publishing the name of the laboratory head on articles. Moreover, he wrote, it would be wrong not to consider the tremendous contribution of

Professor James Collip. Without him, they would certainly not have come up with insulin pure enough to treat diabetes patients. Without the work of a team, such results would have never been achieved.

Banting's response was more bitter. He recalled the frustration after the New Haven meeting, McLeod's lukewarm confidence in his idea; he stated that without the help of Professor Henderson, he would not have been able to work in decent conditions. As for Collip, Banting didn't have much to say. He acknowledged that he had helped, but only once the experiments were well advanced. However, he had only praise for the work of his student, Charles Best.

As for Best himself, perhaps because of his youth, he was more direct about the causes of the dispute. He recognised Bert's skills and his work to improve the quality of the extraction and assay methods. But he rather regretted that Bert and Prof. McLeod had somewhat taken credit for results he himself had obtained. But he was only a student, and did not have a say.

Reconciliation was simply not possible. Banting and McLeod hated each other, as Banting hated his clinician counterpart, Campbell.

~ *CHAPTER 19* ~

In science there are always detractors who for reasons that are both good and bad, do not accept the success of others. Again, the British were no exception. This time, the charge came from Roberts, of the *British Medical Journal*. He criticised Fred and Charley's experiments, their methods and their interpretation of the results. He wrote in the same style as the experts who review articles submitted to scientific journals. But the attack was fierce and presented only the negative aspects. We all agreed with Charley: Fred should not under any circumstances be made aware of the article, especially as it had been written by an Englishman who, moreover, started out by denouncing Fred's hypothesis.

Luckily, Fred was so absorbed in his clinical activities that he never became aware of the article. In addition, Henry Dale published a reply in the next issue of the same journal. Essentially, he maintained that it was not the first time in the history of science that an idea whose foundation was still fragile had given rise to a great discovery, as in the case of insulin, described as 'a major discovery of this century'.

Though certain colleagues, especially scientists, displayed a suspicious attitude, it was quite a different story among the doctors and the press. At a convention in Toronto, their work was greeted with another standing ovation. They had to answer many interviewers' questions, an exercise that Fred, shy and unsure of himself, did not excel in, and above all did not like. Politicians, too, began to show an interest. A reception was organised in Ottawa by the Prime Minister. He had got wind of the quarrels and stormy relationships between the discoverers. It was up to him to find a political solution, because obviously Canada, a Dominion of England, had to honour its best and brightest, whether they hailed from Ontario or Alberta. The message was clear. The Europeans, in turn, got involved by holding a reception for King George V. Too bad I was not invited! I could have swaggered a little before General Monash.

Charley and I suggested to Fred that he might dress a little more smartly for the occasion. His old black suit was worn and shiny, but we stopped short at taking him by the hand to the tailor's. He did not care about his appearance, especially since journalists liked to talk about the penurious situation of researchers.

The University of Toronto had decided to set up a medical research chair that would finally offer Fred a decent salary. As for Charley, he got a scholarship. He was lucky, I could not help remarking. Sure?

"Charley, you're starting to make others jealous. A 5th year student who hasn't even finished his education but receives a big enough scholarship to paint the town red every night..."

"You're right. What's more, Margaret's parents are leaving us their cottage on Lake Simcoe, near here. We're planning to spend a few days there. Why don't you join us? I'm sure you don't know the area around Toronto. Besides, Margaret invited a girlfriend, a Québécoise. You could speak French together... and say bad things about us because we won't understand."

It is hard to imagine a more beautiful sight than a lake where Canada geese start their flight south, and ducks and majestic swans add a dash of colour to the water's glassy surface. The leaves had fallen and covered the roads with enchanting hues. The house on the water, the wooden dock and the boat trip were heaven on Earth. The cottage was aptly named Holiday House. I had just met Louise. She had arrived from Quebec City. I had never heard that very particular way of speaking French. Not an accent, or at any rate hers was light, but particular phrases. She studied physics at Laval University. She talked about the charm of her town perched on the banks of the St. Lawrence River, a city of pirates, much like Saint Malo. Alas, I had not been to St. Malo, I had not even been to Paris, and yet I had spent time in France. Nothing I could say about the country was very exciting, though. Charred trees, the smell of gas, so different from our surroundings at the Ontario lake we were visiting now.

Some of Margaret's and Charley's other friends joined us. It was a festive student atmosphere, giddy with music and dance. I danced the Charleston, not without difficulty though. Louise and I sang French songs that our parents had taught us. Charley preferred traditional American songs and spirituals. Three nights passed this way. I learned more about Louise. She told me about the breakthroughs being made in new physics, especially nuclear physics; the disintegration of atoms, the work of Curie and Rutherford on radioactivity. They had to find molecules, as we did in our research. She invited me to Quebec. She also planned to spend a few months in Stockholm for work experience.

I did not know then how much my life would change because of her.

~ *CHAPTER 20* ~

While we savoured our days at the cottage, Fred was at a conference in Edinburgh with Professor McLeod, who had been invited to give the plenary lecture. He praised the work of all the team members. Even Fred ("that funny character," a young Australian student named Howard Florey said to his neighbour) recognised the quality of McLeod's presentation. In turn, Fred presented the recent data on insulin in the blood. A delegation from the Karolinska Institute in Stockholm was in the audience, unbeknown to Professor McLeod and Fred.

Every autumn, the Nobel Committee meets at the Karolinska Institute to discuss the prize in physiology and medicine. As usual, proposals were made and reports from around the world read and commented upon. The committee arrived at the proposals submitted for the discovery of insulin.

"Some of us have heard about this remarkable discovery made by researchers at the University of Toronto. The hormone called insulin, extracted from the pancreas of animals, could save many human lives; so many people suffer from diabetes. Insulin can reduce glucose and urine ketones. The discovery is the work of Professor John James Rickard McLeod and Dr. Frederick Grant Banting."

"We recently attended the Edinburgh congress and were impressed by the results that were presented."

"But the work was only published early this year. Don't you think the discovery's too new and that it would be wrong to rush it?"

"Especially since for years other researchers, not in Toronto, also suggested the pancreas could release a molecule that acts on blood sugar."

"And the relations between the Toronto researchers are not the most serene."

"Gentlemen, for now I beg you to consider only the scientific aspects. Let us ask ourselves two questions: does this discovery represent a major advance in our fund of knowledge? Does it deserve the Prize? Here we have the reports of professors Crile, Benedict, Stewart and Krogh."

The reports left no doubt. The discovery of insulin was an extraordinary development in endocrinology, opening a vast field of experimentation on the internal secretions of the body. Moreover, despite some aspects of the results and experiments, which to date had not allowed for a pure and well-characterised substance, the report-writers were unanimous in saying the discovery, through its clinical applications already realised, directly coincided with the wishes of Alfred Nobel, 'a discovery that provides the greatest benefit to mankind'.

"Do we agree that this discovery, even if it appears to merit further investigation, meets the committee's expectations?"

"Is anyone against it?"

"I must confess," replied one member, "I am still a little confused. The results are not yet firmly established. This committee must not be forced to acknowledge error at a later date due to a hasty decision."

"But honourable colleague, what about the patients reported

cured, not only in Canada but also in Copenhagen, various American states and even England?"

"Well, I hope those people are actually cured."

"As far as that goes, we have more perspective than for the experiments conducted on animals; I hope you are aware of that, honourable colleague?"

"I am confused as to who exactly the recipients would be."

"Honourable colleague that is point number two. For the first point, do you agree with the majority of our colleagues and experts?"

"I am obliged to respond in the affirmative."

"Thank you. Now let us move on to the second question. Who would like to speak? The debate is open."

Several opinions were expressed. Agreement was quickly reached on the name of Banting. The idea came from him and he actually treated patients. As for Professor McLeod, as one expert report stated, he was criticised by several members for being nothing more than the group's manager, having built his reputation in quite another field. Furthermore, if, as the expert claimed, the experiments were not always conducted correctly, the director had to bear at least partial responsibility for that.

"But without technical, financial and material assistance from Professor McLeod, and also his discerning viewpoint, people would still be dying of this horrible disease… the sight of those skeletal people reminds us of dreadful scenes from the recent war."

"Please do not mix science and politics," said one member.

"So, my esteemed colleagues, do you think that Dr. Frederick Banting alone deserves the Nobel Prize, or should we present it in association with Professor John McLeod?"

There was a long silence.

"I see the two names have been chosen by the majority."

"What about three names?" a solemn voice said. "I suggest Prof. R. Pfeiffer, the German bacteriologist who in the 1890s discovered the cause of influenza." The speaker was the man who had confessed to confusion about the founders of insulin.

The committee chairman spoke again.

"Other committee members do not feel it is possible to have three names, or present a prize on two different themes. This has never been done before and is not a good idea. We will submit our proposal for both names and our recommendations to the Nobel Assembly."

It took several days and many return trips for the nineteen wise men of the Karolinska Institute to finally vote by secret ballot that the Nobel Prize in Physiology or Medicine be awarded to Frederick Banting and John McLeod.

~ *PART THREE* ~

~ *CHAPTER 21* ~

The Nobel Committee had not expected its decision to cause such a stir in the Toronto laboratory.

Fred arrived back from his parents' home in Alliston. He had not read the papers or listened to the radio. I went to meet him.

"Fred, we've been looking for you everywhere! Have you read the papers?"

"Do you think I've got nothing better to do? I drew up the plans for an extension for my parents' house, and then spent over an hour driving the Model T up a steep hill by the Nottawasaga River. I hadn't put in enough gas, and the fuel could not reach the engine, so I had to drive in reverse. It took me a whole hour to get up the damn hill! I built up quite a sweat!"

"Okay, but have you read the papers?"

"Why would I, you know I can't stand journalists!"

"Do you want me to tell you the news?"

"What news?"

"You've won the Nobel Prize."

"No! I don't believe you!"

He burst into tears against my shoulder.

"Uh... with McLeod."

"What?"

Fred stormed down the hall towards the lab, uttering all the insults that came to his head.

"I'll send a telegram to Stockholm. I don't want this prize. No part of this discovery came out of McLeod's brain."

"Calm down. I'll bring you a beer and you can think it over. You're going to listen to me now, me, the young medic from the trenches of the Somme. You're going to stop this nonsense. You went to fight in France: why? For your country, wasn't it? So think about it. You're the first Canadian to receive the Nobel Prize. Have you thought about that? What will people think of a cranky researcher and of research in general if you refuse? And have you thought about your parents, your family, the honour you'll bring them? And the town of Alliston that will be so proud of its native son? Your university that supported you and friends like Charley?"

"Where is he, so I can congratulate him?"

"In Boston, as you well know. He's speaking to students at Harvard."

"That's right, he told me that. Can you send him a telegram right away?"

"Start dictating."

"Charley, read this as soon as you get it, sitting down. The Nobel Prize has been awarded to McLeod and myself. I want to share it with you, even if they forgot to name you for all your worthy contributions to the discovery of insulin."

Fred had time to calm down before Professor McLeod returned from Scotland. The professor was met by a swarm of reporters on his arrival in Montreal on November 2, 1923. He had learned that Fred wanted to share his prize with Charley.

"This award is for a team," Professor McLeod answered a

journalist's question. "The Nobel Committee cannot thank all of us. So I decided to share my prize endowment with Professor James Bertram Collip of the University of Alberta, thanks to whom we were able to have the insulin that can be administered to patients and cure them."

Banting and McLeod wrote the Nobel Committee that they could not attend the awards ceremony in December but would send their speeches. Everyone understood that it was not possible for either Banting or McLeod to attend the ceremony without their animosity becoming obvious to everyone. The University of Toronto was unhappy about it, and the politicians even more so.

That night, I awoke with a start. What a great opportunity this would be to see Louise! She had just left for Stockholm. I discussed my idea with Professor McLeod, asking him to give me time off to explore Europe, about which I knew so little. It was my lucky day; Professor McLeod even offered to finance my transatlantic voyage.

The December cold in Sweden was just as biting as in Canada, even more so. The streets of Stockholm were covered with snow. Christmas decorations were already up. It wasn't very far from the home of Santa Claus. People moved around the streets on skis; others skated on the many lakes and rivers of ice that crisscrossed the peaceful Swedish capital. The language was incomprehensible. Tall, elegant silhouettes glided by, hidden under their warm fur caps, their '*tuques*' as Louise called them. She lived in a small one-room flat on campus. In her letters, she often compared Quebec City and Stockholm, due to the European culture, no doubt.

The hardest part was finding a tuxedo for the ceremony. It reminded me of the day I had to drag Fred into a store to make him buy a new suit. But this time, I had a woman with me. It was obvious that the saleswoman was curious about us, two young people a long way from home.

"Have you come for a wedding?" she asked in perfect English.

"Not entirely. More a kind of reconciliation," I answered without thinking.

I kept checking to make sure I still had the two precious invitations that Professor McLeod and Fred had given me.

The ceremony took place on December 10, 1923, with the King of Sweden in attendance. It was spectacular. Due to the heat of the royal hall (or maybe my tuxedo was too tight) I almost felt as if I were hallucinating. I imagined Dr. Frederick Banting and Professor John McLeod standing with the other recipients: Fritz Pregl, Austrian Nobel Prize in Chemistry for his studies on the microanalysis of organic substances, Robert Millikan, American Nobel laureate in physics for the photoelectric effect, and the Irish poet William Yeats, all of whom were actually there. And then I imagined General John Monash in their midst, in military uniform. Why shouldn't he have been awarded a Nobel too, for bringing the war to an end, preventing it from going on endlessly in the trenches and causing millions of deaths? But it was unthinkable to give the Nobel Peace Prize to a general. Too bad. He too had quarrelled with his British superiors, with Hughes, the Prime Minister... But that would not have prevented him from getting the award!

Louise looked at me, sensing that something was amiss. She saw I was weeping, listening to Professor Sjöquist, the awards committee spokesman, who movingly recalled the work of Claude Bernard on glycogen and sugar formation, and thus, indirectly, the work of his students, including my godfather

Paul Bert, whom I had been named after. Professor Sjöquist made sure to mention the contribution of each and every researcher. Perhaps for the award recipients, discovering insulin had been a matter of seizing a fortunate opportunity; but as Louis Pasteur said, "fortune favours only the prepared mind."

~ *CHAPTER 22* ~

I had learned a lot during these two years in Toronto. I had discovered the fascinating profession of research. With its high points, when the results confirm an idea that has been germinating and pondered for months; and also its low points, when nothing works out as hoped, and must be started over again and again. Slave labour, without respite, without rest. But you needed optimism to do this job, and sometimes fortune smiled upon you. Sometimes you were there at the right moment, when a great discovery was made, and were able to say you had been part of it. What an honour and a joy!

I also learned this world of research, like that of medicine, believed to bring knowledge or improve well-being, was no different from the society in which we lived. Power, ambition, and self-regard make for difficult relations. But, fortunately, research is not only made of conflict but of shared enthusiasm, friendship and a life of freedom that is incomparably rich.

The quarrels between these men in Toronto were sheer silliness compared to the ordeals of war I had known. I had rubbed shoulders with those who had attained the great consecration, the Holy Grail, the Nobel Prize, yet their childish behaviour sometimes irritated me.

Friendship, like love, does not follow a continuous line. It fluctuates with time, but it lasts. Together Charley and I had written up our Master's reports, his for the University of Toronto, mine for Melbourne. Again, how fortunate to be able to tell a story, an extraordinary story which had resulted in the saving of lives. Naturally, our manuscripts were mainly focused on the development of techniques used routinely in the laboratory: the preparation of extracts, the development of methods for measuring glucose and ketones in the blood and urine, liver glycogen and the respiratory quotient. As for the more clinical aspects of the effects of insulin, we had to keep those for the MD. We had agreed that it was appropriate to describe the results without specifying whether the improvements were derived from one group or the other. We felt that the interpersonal conflicts had lasted long enough.

Seven years had passed since I had left Toronto to go back to Melbourne. Charley had gone to England with Margaret on a postdoctoral fellowship at Henry Dale's lab. They had married just before I left in 1924. Back in Toronto, he became head of the laboratory. Professor McLeod, no doubt tired of all the quarrelling, had decided to return to Scotland, to the University of Aberdeen. Fred had also married and had a son, Bill, who would soon be two years old. His wife, Marion, liked large receptions, which Fred hated. He continued to work with diabetes patients, devoting himself body and soul to treating the disease. He was also interested in working on cancer, but met with little success. He was increasingly passionate about painting. Landscapes fascinated him. Every trip he took was an opportunity to do new paintings. He brought all the necessary equipment with him to Quebec, the French Riviera, the castles of the Loire, and the Ontario farms he loved so much... like

Jane's, across from his parents' farm; Jane, his childhood friend, carried off by diabetes at fourteen. Fred had never forgotten her. He had not forgotten me either. He sent me postcards of the Amiens battlefields in the Somme, and of the Folies Bergeres in Paris. A trip around Europe before Stockholm, where he would make his Nobel Prize presentation to the audience from the Karolinska Institute.

Bert Collip had decided to specialise in hormones. He was right, I think. It was the field of the future. We kept in close touch and each of his letters revealed his passion for research. He had discovered a new hormone in the parathyroid gland, a molecule that could regulate calcium. To my surprise, he had left Alberta with his family to settle in Westmount, an English-speaking area of Montreal, having accepted an offer from McGill University to head the Department of Biochemistry.

Louise had also returned to Quebec City. With a PhD in Physics under her belt, she would most certainly get a position at Laval University. In all these years, despite my insistence, she had never come to Australia. "It's too long a trip," she said, "I can't leave for such a long time."

Our long letters crossed the ocean waves. They always ended with passionate words of love. I missed her terribly.

Our correspondence became my only link with the French language. I had always spoken French with my parents, but then, one after the other, they passed away. My mother probably died of a disease contracted in the hospital where she worked, my father in a senseless accident, hit by a car on King Street.

I was alone for a long time. My friend Mac left for London after his medical degree to train in bacteriology. He married Edith. It was probably on Mac's recommendation that the director of the Walter and Eliza Hall Institute of Bacteriology in Melbourne invited me to continue my research along with my clinical activities in endocrinology. I, too, had finally set my heart on the study of hormones. But I was bored in Melbourne. Was it because of bacteriology, which I found interesting but not really exciting? Was it the geographical remoteness of Australia, the death of my parents or, more recently, that of John Monash? He died of pneumonia at the age of sixty-six – "a reasonable age," people said. A huge crowd accompanied him to the Jewish cemetery where he was buried next to Vic. The 'diggers' were all there to pay tribute to the national hero, who had not received the Nobel Prize.

And I missed Louise. Terribly.

It was the end of 1931. In his most recent letter, Bert wrote that he was looking for an assistant to help him with the purification of new hormones extracted from the pituitary gland.

'Paul, if you know a biochemist somewhere, let me know. I haven't had much luck here in Montreal'.

My answer was immediate – and ironic.

'Dear Bert, sir, Mr. Professor, do you think I may be allowed to apply for the job? I learned biochemistry a few years ago with a competent, honest and courageous man. He purified the miracle cure whose benefits I witness every day in my daily practice. But perhaps you don't want any more doctors around? Too pretentious, cocky and dismissive?'

I received a response a few weeks later, this time sent by air mail.

Dear Paul, I thought research had lost you forever and the clinic swallowed you up! Don't be silly, if you want to come, I welcome you with open arms. Who else would I take on if not you? Naturally with a much higher salary than that of a simple assistant. I'll immediately apply to the immigration authorities. As a citizen of a Dominion, you'll have no problem getting a work permit, and with your Military Cross, it will be even easier. Do you want one permit or more?

Your friend, Bert.

PS: You've told me nothing about your love life. What's the latest?

I wondered if I should tell him that my main reason for returning to Canada was to see Louise, to be with her.

~ *CHAPTER 23* ~

Australia really was the ends of the Earth! I was growing repelled by those long boat trips. I needed to occupy myself. Since I had become a doctor, it had been a ritual to inform the captain that I was willing, if necessary, to help the doctor on duty. And on every one of my voyages, it was necessary. My father told me he had met my mother on his first trip to Australia. There was a priest who wanted to exorcise an epileptic. My father sent him back to his missal. There was nothing like that this time, but the journey was long.

Finally we reached the majestic St. Lawrence River. Our boat made its way through the blocks of ice that were just beginning to melt. The entire landscape around the river was white, a blanket of snow covering all the fields and houses. Silence. An island ahead. We left it to our right. Then waterfalls of a dizzying height, trapped in ice, a translucent mountain.

"Montmorency Falls," a sailor said. "We just passed Ile d'Orleans."

Good French names. And then, before us, a rocky outcrop, smoke rising above it from houses and factory chimneys. And at last, a city: Quebec. The closer we got, the more I agreed with Louise – the site was incomparable. The houses with their colourful roofs reminded me of pictures in the books of my childhood. The Château Frontenac, with its multiple green roofs, loomed over the city and Cap Diamant, like an old feudal castle. My ticket was for Montreal, but I could not go any further. I had to get off, right away, and end my voyage there. I could not resist, I had to see Louise, immediately.

Our boat made a stopover in Quebec City. I explained to the ship's doctor why I wanted to end my journey.

"Do you have your papers?"

"Yes, but they're for Montreal and Immigration is there."

"Come with me. I think we can get you by quite easily. Pack your things. We'll put them with the luggage of the passengers getting off here. I'll see you in ten minutes."

I was very anxious during the formalities. A rather frail-looking man in uniform with a strong English Canadian accent asked us what our business was in Québec.

"Just a little tour of the city with my colleague," said the ship's doctor. "He's never been to Québec and we have a two hour wait."

"Do you have your papers?"

"Yes of course."

The man looked me up and down.

"And what about you?" He scanned my working papers for Canada.

"You can't get out here, sir; you'll have to go through Immigration in Montreal."

"Let him through," said the doctor. "His lady love is here."

"The law is the law. There's nothing I can do."

The man kept looking at me insistently and then suddenly began to speak English.

"I've seen you somewhere... Have you been to Canada?"

"Yes, I went to the University of Toronto."

"That's where I've seen you before! I'm from that region and I was treated for diabetes by Professor Banting."

"I actually worked with him."

"So it's you who found the miracle of insulin that saved my life?"

"Yes, I think so."

"Thank you! Thank you with all my heart. Go on, I never saw you."

And so I found myself in Canada, having bypassed Immigration. My colleague could not believe it. I told him my story briefly over a beer in a bar in Lower Town, while waiting for my luggage.

I had Louise's address. Galipeault Road. She had told me it was near the Plains of Abraham where the French had abandoned the French Canadians against the English in a cowardly manner in 1760.

I took one of those carriages – *calèches* – that you see all over the old city. Galipeault Road was a little outside of the city walls. The building was red brick, three stories high, with a covered terrace on the ground floor.

"Hello, may I ask if this the home of Louise Leblanc?"

"Our professor? Yes she lives here. But she isn't back yet. At this hour, she must still be at the university."

"Can I leave my luggage with you?"

"No problem. *Vous avez eu donc ben d'la misère à porter tout cà icitte?*"[1]

I had a little trouble following.

---

[1]You must have had a wretched time hauling that stuff all this way!

"Do you know where she works?"

"*D'icitte vous sortez à gauche, vous frappez une lumière. Un quart de mile et vous vous droppez sur Cartier.*"[2]

If you can move easily from English to French, you manage to get the drift of the idiom and the accent. I was so happy that I kept laughing to myself. I did not even feel the cold. Everything in the town was beautiful. The people were cheerful and friendly.

"Is this the Physics building?"

"May I help you? Who are you looking for?" said an assistant who was much more amiable than the one who had received me on my arrival at the lab in Toronto.

"Louise Leblanc."

"She should be in her office, just down the hall."

In the seconds that preceded the long-awaited moment, our entire past returned to my memory. I felt anxious again. How would she react? She wasn't expecting to see me. Suddenly I was filled with doubt. She probably would not appreciate me arriving unannounced like this. Standing in front of the closed door, I hesitated to knock. What if everything suddenly fell apart?

---

[2] From here, go left and you'll hit a traffic light. Quarter of a mile further and you'll land on Cartier Road.

~ *CHAPTER 24* ~

Nothing had changed between us. She looked as if she had simply been waiting for me to open her door one day and take her in my arms. I had so much to tell her. I sent a telegram to Bert to say I'd be arriving in Montreal in a week. A whole week with Louise, what bliss!

Her flat was a simple room on the ground floor of the building. She shared the kitchen with other tenants, mainly academics. Now that she was going to hold the position of Associate Professor, she was thinking of moving into a larger apartment. The distance between Quebec and Montreal did not compare with the distance from Australia, but still we would be separated again. We promised to see each other every weekend in either city. She loved Montreal, which was livelier than Quebec City. Perhaps she would even consider going to work there.

It took a whole day by train or bus to travel the two hundred miles that lay between us.

When I arrived at the station, Bert was waiting for me. He greeted me warmly.

"I'm glad to see you at last, Paul. We're both going to make new discoveries, I'm sure of it. I found you a nice apartment on

University Street, right downtown, close to McGill. We have superb facilities, very well equipped. I'll drive you there, you'll see."

I saw. I gritted my teeth the whole way. Bert loved driving fast. We crossed Montreal at breakneck speed. Yet the journey lasted longer than expected: we had a flat tyre. The beautiful white front tyre was just a piece of lifeless flaccid rubber. Through bad luck or negligence, the spare tyre was also deflated. Imagine the scene: Bert carrying the damaged wheel at arm's length and me dragging my suitcases behind him. Fortunately, we found a taxi. Bert left the car near a sidewalk. We left the wheel in a garage and it was dark by the time we arrived at my apartment. He had not exaggerated; the apartment was superb with a magnificent view of Mount Royal.

"It's time for supper. We'll go back and get the car. I hope the wheel is fixed. I'll take you to my house. You can meet Ray and the children."

We roared off to Westmount at top speed. Exhausted and in a cold sweat, sitting next to the madman at the wheel, I wondered if I would still have the strength to eat supper.

"If you're scared with me, you will always be scared in a car. Driving is a little like flying, but, alas, not as fast."

I held my breath...

Ray knew everything about me, or almost. My war experience, the purification of insulin with her husband, the tense atmosphere of the Toronto lab. But that was the past. In Alberta, Bert had achieved everything he had wanted to. Was he not part of the great team that had worked on insulin? He was recognised by his peers and had enough money to do his work properly: support from donations, contracts and royalties for the discovery of insulin.

I said goodnight to Ray. The children were in bed. Bert insisted on driving me home. To avoid looking at the road, I started talking.

"Why did you come to Montreal? Why did you leave Edmonton where you had everything you'd asked for? You never told me."

"You know, in research you always need to have a guide. Someone you can follow. Someone whose merit and skills you recognise. I am very grateful to my mentor, Professor Archibald Macallum. He taught me everything about biochemistry techniques. Then he left Edmonton for McGill. I had been contacted by the President of McGill to come assist Professor Macallum. I refused at first because Ray didn't want us to leave with three young children. So as you know, I became interested in a new endocrine gland, the parathyroids. I redid the same experiments as those we had performed on pancreatic extracts, again with success. I was able to isolate a substance, the parathyroid hormone."

"And I also read that someone named Hanson attacked you, claiming he'd discovered that hormone before you and treated people," I said.

"It's true, and I suffered a lot. But it was more an issue of big money than a real scientific feud. Hanson had an agreement with Parke-Davis Company, which, as you know, is a competitor of Eli Lilly. Then we had some controversy via scientific journals. It was only recently the lawyers settled the litigation, recognizing that even if Hanson actually produced active parathyroid extracts, we were the ones who showed that our purified extracts made it possible to regulate calcium levels. And that was thanks to an improved detection technique that I had developed with Clark. And above all, we emphasised that this was the cause of tetany. You see, it's like with Fred…

clinicians observe an effect, but they can't explain it. By the way, I've had a nice office set up for you, with a view of Mount Royal, like your apartment. You'll find everything you need there."

"And so then you agreed to come to Montreal?"

"Yes, with Professor Macallum retiring, I agreed to succeed him, out of gratitude... and also for the salary and the opportunity of living in Quebec."

On entering my office, I found a stack of articles with a note on top:

I couldn't send all this to you in Australia, so take your time to read these articles. If you come across an idea you think is wise, well, it's yours. My best. Bert.

~ *CHAPTER 25* ~

"You know, Bert, I don't think this is the time to talk about extracts. It's better to study the hormones themselves. They act as information transmitters."

"I quite agree with you, the study of hormones is the future. But do we at least know where they come from? And what diseases they are involved in?"

"Hard to believe that you, of all people, are talking like this! A clinician! Aren't we entitled to believe that in healthy humans, these hormones have a fundamental role?"

"Such as?"

"The pituitary. Small gland at the base of the brain that probably contains a large quantity of hormones. In reading some of these articles, I formed an opinion on it."

"Yes, but if you're right, we'll have to isolate and purify those hormones."

"Well, that's a good research topic, isn't it? I tell you, Bert, the pituitary is the master gland of the body."

"Then prove it. Personally, I have another focal point: placenta hormones. Especially because they seem very different from pituitary hormones."

I met Arthur Long, who had come from Alberta with Bert to handle the necessary administration of the laboratory. Then there was David Thomson, an assistant professor from England, with a distinctly British style who had spent several months in France, and of course, Roscoff and Grenoble. A voracious reader, he knew everything published on the subject of hormones.

He was in charge of teaching, which freed me up to do research full-time. They were all working on placenta hormones. Emmenin, for example, a steroid taken by mouth that could treat reproductive disorders. A discovery that promoted the well-being of women, a discovery "for the good of humanity" as Alfred Nobel would have said.

I felt a little alone with my rat pituitaries, very small compared with the tons of placenta that arrived at the lab. But everything was about to change. Students in biology and medicine at McGill had naturally heard of our lab's success. Despite the difficulties caused by the Great Depression, we had money to operate and recruit technicians, all thanks to Bert's close ties with the pharmaceutical industry. There were animated discussions every day, around the 'boss'. At four in the afternoon, we shared a ritual cup of tea. A bell announced to all of us that tea was served. It was a time to meet, to discuss and to exchange ideas, everything you needed to create a serene and joyful atmosphere. The tradition had originated with Professor Macallum, this *art de vivre* and freedom in the way of conducting research. The results came so easily that publications soon followed. Bert was fascinated by chemistry experiments. He rejoiced at the noise of the extraction machinery in the lab. He marvelled like a child, moving from one extractor to another to watch the fluids forming. He did not worry about the danger of the organic solvents used. He constantly smoked long cigarettes that he rolled himself, leaving trails of ash in his wake; you could always see where he had been. He often left the lab late at night. It is true that, given the way he drove, he got home quickly.

On weekends, he frequently brought his daughter Barbara to the lab. When I was there, he settled her in my office. I learned to play house and draw Mickey Mouse, a recent creation by Walt Disney, and supervise homework.

One evening, while I was observing pituitary tissue under the microscope, Bert entered.

"Paul, I have just received a letter from a young Austrian or German doctor, I don't know exactly. He studied in Prague, and spent a year at Johns Hopkins in Baltimore. He works on parathyroid hormone and wants to do a postdoctoral fellowship here. Can I suggest that he work with you?"

"Why not? There aren't many of us working on the pituitary. All of you are more interested in the placenta."

"What can you do? That's what the boss wants!" he said, laughing.

As he had done for me, and certainly for everyone who wanted to work in the lab, Bert made every effort to help the new recruit. He even arranged the work permits with the Immigration authorities, as well as the housing and salary. For this postdoctoral student, a young doctor of twenty-five, things were a little different. He had a fellowship from the Rockefeller Foundation. And so, in April of 1932, Hans Selye arrived at the lab.

~ *CHAPTER 26* ~

Once more, Bert was right. Hans turned out to be the rare bird we had been looking for. We complemented each other. He knew anatomy, histology, and had the finely skilled hands required for microsurgery. Right from the first minutes, something happened between us, though I cannot quite say what. One sometimes has the impression that there is no need to talk, explain or make oneself understood. Hans was younger than me, he was only twenty-five, and he already had several publications to his credit, in German.

"How could you already be publishing on your own?"

"It's a tradition with us. At the University of Prague, you have to publish your papers for your doctorate. And we publish them in German, because it is a German-speaking university."

"But you are German, aren't you?"

"No, my father is Hungarian, a military doctor. My mother is Austrian. They both wanted to give us a good education. I grew up in Komarom, a funny town that has been divided by a river for the past ten years. One side is Hungary, the other Czechoslovakia. My father was not very happy with my choice of doing research instead of a medical career."

"Oh, neither was mine. He wondered how a doctor could possibly become a biologist."

"What does your father do?"

"He died not long ago. He was a professor of neurology at the University of Melbourne. My mother was a doctor too, of Irish origin."

"So you're not Canadian?"

"No, Australian, and as a matter of fact, I served in the war against the Germans."

"But weren't you too young?"

"Yes, but I was committed to following an Australian general, the one who paved the way for German defeat in northern France."

"And do you speak other languages besides English?"

"Yes, French. Again because of my father. He was French and went to Australia for his work, and also to follow in my grandfather's footsteps. And he became Australian."

"If you want, we can speak French together. I love the French language, and you can correct my mistakes. After all, we're in Montreal, the most European city in North America, right?"

"I suppose so. What makes you say that?"

"You know, if I left Baltimore and the Johns Hopkins lab, it's not because I wasn't interested in the research they were doing, but because I missed Europe, its lifestyle and culture. My scholarship from the Rockefeller Foundation required that I stay on the North American continent for a while yet. That is why I wrote to Professor Collip and asked him if I could come here for six months, since I'd worked a little on hormones."

That is how, in only a few months, two foreign postdoctoral associates who worked on the pituitary gland changed the lab's orientation. Hans brought his surgical skills to the work, and I took care of the biochemical part. Hans had read the papers of Philip Smith, who worked in Herbert Evans's laboratory in Berkeley, California. He had developed a new surgical approach for removing the pituitary gland of a rat and keeping the animal alive. In a very short time Hans had tackled and improved this surgical technique. In less than five minutes he was able to perform an hypophysectomy, the name given to this operation. That is how we came to have hundreds of animals that we had operated upon and could use to test our tissue extracts. Hans operated with great dexterity. As an anatomist and histologist, he was able to observe the consequences of hypophysectomy on various tissues, and the effects of the extracts. We ended up persuading Bert that pituitary hormones were just as important as PLA, the placental hormone on which he worked more specifically.

With this new technique, we were able to obtain extracts that made it possible to restore reproductive functions, those of the thyroid gland and of what in laboratory terminology is called the pituitary-adrenal axis. Then Evelyn Anderson joined us from Evans's Laboratory, and we were able to isolate the thyroid hormone and the adrenocorticotrophic hormone, which protects against the reduction in size, due to hypophysectomy, of the small glands located above the kidney, the adrenal glands.

Of course, scientific rivalry soon ensued. Evans had started work on the pituitary before Bert. He had developed an hypophysectomy technique that was different from ours and did not give the animals the same chance of survival. Evans had also isolated a pituitary hormone that stimulated milk production and probably two different hormones that acted upon the ovary. The competition between scientists had begun.

For fear of in-house spying, we avoided saying too much to Evelyn. I learned how to proceed so as not to disclose important information. Hans went as far as writing his articles in German to ensure that the US group did not understand the intricacies of the scientific process. But the relations between Evans and Bert were not as strained as they had been between the insulin researchers in Toronto years before. Discussions focused solely on scientific, not personal issues. Both men were genuine pioneers of modern endocrinology. They were aware of the need to develop large laboratories, to train researchers with multiple and complementary skills, and the essential aim was to understand the secrets of life.

~ *CHAPTER 27* ~

Hans had to return to Prague. His scholarship had expired. I went to see Bert.

"Bert, you can't let Hans go! He's absolutely vital to the laboratory. It's true that others here are beginning to master hypophysectomy, but Hans has core competencies in physiology that we definitely do not possess. If you want to keep the edge over Evans, you mustn't let Hans go."

"You know him well. Do you think he'd like to stay?"

"I think so. In fact, I'm sure. He is very keen on these new discoveries. I don't think he wants to give it all up."

"I'll see what I can do. Right now, I need to find him an assistantship. You know I will not tolerate lack of job security. Research has become a true profession. And all work deserves a salary."

Bert was not long in finding the necessary funding. The President of McGill agreed. He could refuse Bert nothing, and nor could the Carnegie Foundation. All that remained was to complete the necessary formalities to create a job in Canada. Bert took care of that too.

And so, after spending some time in Prague, Hans returned to Montreal, and this time he knew it was for good.

Articles were published one after the other, many with young Hans Selye as first author, in the *Proceedings of the Society for Experimental Biology*. Every time an article came out, we drank Tokaj, either a bottle brought back by Hans in his luggage or one that had been sent to him from Hungary. With a score of publications each year, quite a number of bottles were consumed.

As Hans was the youngest, he was the one Bert sent to get cow ovaries from the slaughterhouse. Hans had refused to be driven by Bert, but to get Bert to agree he had to invent quite a ploy. He was not the only one who feared Bert's driving. One student even said during a celebration for the end of his thesis, "We don't always remember what was written in the articles, but a car trip with Professor Collip we remember all our lives!"

We enjoyed several years of success that opened the way for significant progress in the study of hormones. Meanwhile our personal lives became chaotic. We could not all be like Bert, living only for research, especially since we were young and had other interests.

I tried to spend a weekend in Quebec City with Louise every fortnight. And she sometimes came to Montreal, mostly for work. I arranged to be free when she was there. That is no doubt one of the most attractive aspects of research: being free, free to choose what we wanted to work on and take the time we needed.

The laboratory on the third floor of the Biology building had become too small. As the university in Toronto had done for Fred, McGill would have to build a new institute for Bert, an institute of endocrinology. Despite the difficulties caused by the Depression, there were still sufficient funds to provide for this kind of construction. The university, but also the government and a number of foundations were able to contribute the necessary financing. But McGill University management was greedy. It asked for more and more money, often to invest, rather than use to finance the advance of science. The Rockefeller Foundation was ready to pay for the construction of the building, but the conditions stipulated by McGill were unacceptable. Every possible pretext was used to criticise Collip's work and justify the Foundation's refusal to finance the project. However, scientific programmes, less costly for the Foundation, would receive their assistance. One of these was a new laboratory project on anti-hormones. Hans, ever curious, became interested. We had observed that some animals had stopped responding after repeated administrations of hormones. Bert and Hans believed that the blood could synthesise substances that acted as antibodies to block the effects of these hormones. The subject naturally gave rise to debate. Was it a good or a false lead? We were not able to isolate antagonistic principles in the blood, and yet it was possible to detect resistance to hormone injections in humans. Hans did not acknowledge that it was possible to doubt observations proved by experiment.

This indeed was the case with ovary extracts obtained from slaughterhouses, injected into rats, whose sex organs were then observed by Hans.

"Paul, can you tell me if you see the same difference as I do between this animal and that one?"

"It is clear that her ovaries and her uterus are much bigger."

"Is that all?"

"That's quite a lot, isn't it?"

"Biochemists are very poor observers."

"What do you mean?"

"Look harder."

"I can't see anything."

"You are exasperating, Paul. Look at the adrenal glands, they're also enlarged, and see the ulceration of the stomach and intestine?"

"That's true, but I think those are artefacts."

"Artefacts... listen, we'll inject extracts from other organs and different substances and we'll see."

At first, without talking to Bert, we actually discovered some surprising things. We always observed the same changes, whether with the other extracts or toxic substances.

"You see perfectly well that this can't be just an experimental artefact. You're really getting on my nerves, Paul, with your artefacts. How can I prove to you that every time an animal is attacked it responds in the same way, with morphological changes that may be related to hormonal secretions? I have an idea."

It was a brilliant idea that could well have got us expelled from the university. It was the middle of winter. It was snowing and cold, perhaps even colder than usual. Hans put a cage of rats outside. The unfortunate animals did not survive but we could see that their symptoms were similar to those observed after the injections. This experiment might have gone unnoticed if Hans had not had the wild idea of taking the rats to the top of the building. On the roof of the Biology building was a siren. Hans had developed a system that made it possible to set it off remotely. It wailed in the mid-afternoon as if to warn the population of impending bombardment. The whole university flocked outside. People ran terrified in all directions in search of shelter. Minutes later, the police arrived, the army right behind them.

The culprits were quickly identified. They had left clear traces... rats. We were summoned by the administration. It took a show of diplomacy and intervention from Bert and Professor Martin, Dean of the faculty, to explain that those experiments were essential. A diplomatic but necessary lie in order to save the day, because in reality Bert was already angry with Hans. Bert was opposed to this type of experiment. He found the observations unfounded, unscientific.

~ *CHAPTER 28* ~

The more time passed, the more convinced Hans became of the validity of his theory: that the reaction of the animal was not a response to a specific substance but an alarm response of the body, as when one is ill.

Although they had published an article together in a Canadian journal, Bert and Hans were not in agreement. Bert tried to dissuade Hans from continuing down this road. But Hans was beginning to rebel. He increasingly took umbrage at his master's criticism. He could not bear the fact that only the boss was allowed to have the ideas, the appropriate ones. The tension between the two men was palpable. Bert was aware of everything Hans contributed with regard to the physiological aspects. As for Hans, carried away by the enthusiasm of youth and a certain lack of maturity, he tended to overdo things a little.

"If he wants to do his damned experiments, so be it, but not with this lab's money," Bert told me angrily one day.

The tension was at its height, and I found myself caught between the two. I understood both points of view and tried to reason with them, taking account of Hans's enthusiasm as well as Bert's wisdom.

Louise had come to spend the weekend in Montreal. The weather was miserable, as it often is in Quebec in winter. So much snow that you cannot leave the house. Days so grey and dreary that you feel it would be better to simply stay in bed. And being cooped up in the house alone with Louise for two whole days was something that had not happened in a long time. There had been numerous storm warnings but that had not prevented careless motorists from becoming marooned in the streets. Bert, of course, was one of these. Braving the elements at all costs to get to the laboratory, he rammed straight into a snow bank in Westmount. From all reports, only the rear half of his car was visible. Bert was more frightened than hurt. But sliding around on frozen snow required special equipment, and, despite Bert's passion for cars, his reckless driving was ill suited to winter conditions.

"You look worried, Paul. Is it about the lab?" Louise asked.

"Yes, a little. I'm not very happy with how things are going. Our experiments work beautifully, as I've already said, but the human relations are poisoning the atmosphere. Hans and Bert will not stop bickering. They'll end up hating each other if it continues. I was in this kind of situation in Toronto, and I do not want it to start again. It's always the same story, the teacher and his pupil. The student gains confidence and decides he has to surpass the master. I told Hans he has to learn to control himself and that we're lucky to have a leader like Bert. He gives us free rein but he is there to encourage us, and moreover, he continues to do his own experiments."

"You know, there are personal conflicts everywhere. Not only in biology, in physics too. A laboratory is like a microcosm of society. You might think that in the research community, people are bright enough to avoid this kind of thing. But it's all human nature, the appetite for power, the desire to be better than the others, to possess knowledge and strength... You'll notice it's often men more than women who manage to hate each other so much."

"You don't think women are the same?"

She kissed me, and continued,

"Except there are not as many of them in research and higher education. You have before you a rare specimen, you know, very rare in fact. Maybe it really is a question of hormones, since you like them so much. What if everything depends on testosterone...?"

The discussion amused us, and we were happy lying pressed against each other under the warm duvet, caring very little indeed about who, or what hormone would prevail over the other.

Returning to the lab was even more difficult than usual. Hans, eager to enforce his point of view, constantly tried to solicit my support. Perhaps he thought I could help him to convince Bert.

"You know, Paul, I have great respect for Bert, but when will he understand that my theory is viable? He has only contempt for me now, but one day I'll show him I'm right."

"This reminds me of Banting and McLeod. Or David and Goliath. You know, you have to wait for the right moment."

"But now is the moment, Paul. Dr. Martin has asked me to work in the Department of Anatomy. And I will accept his offer."

"I hope you realise, Hans, that without you, Bert's research will suffer, and mine too. You bring us your irrefutable knowledge of anatomy and histology. And remember, he gave you complete freedom to do your own work. Isn't that worth something?"

"I promise you, Paul, that if I leave the department, I will continue to work with you. I know that Bert is a great researcher and that he developed endocrinology and deserves a Nobel Prize. But what choice do I have? I can't stand people denigrating my work, as if it were nothing but studying artefacts and doing pharmacology's nasty work. How do you explain that an animal resistant to estradiol is also resistant to diethylstilbestrol, a derivative? We did not find any anti-hormones in the blood. Where is the specific nature of the substance Bert is so attached to? I don't understand him; I don't follow him any more."

"Still, Hans, give some thought to the consequences of your departure for all of us."

~ *CHAPTER 29* ~

But still Hans left us. And the vitality of the laboratory was greatly diminished. The great years of exciting discoveries were clearly behind us. Most of the hormones manufactured by that little gland, the pituitary, had been identified, but their effects had yet to be explored in full. Biochemistry, anatomy or histology alone could not tell us more about these hormones. Hans was smart enough not to get on Bert's bad side. He kept his word. Despite his involvement with another university department, they continued to publish papers together and moreover on Hans's subject, although it was disputed by Bert.

Getting out of the lab for a change of scene is sometimes a very good thing. Conventions often help us to think of other things besides daily life in the laboratory. They allow us to meet other researchers, pursue often-animated discussions on research, or simply be among friends.

As it did every year, the Canadian Medical Association was holding a conference. It was an opportunity for our students to meet colleagues from all the universities in Canada, attend presentations on various subjects and sometimes initiate collaborations. The conference that year was being held in

Toronto. I had not been back there since I had left for Montreal, but I remained in contact with Charley. From time to time, Fred sent me long letters that unfortunately were often sad. Since the discovery of insulin and despite the institute that had been built in his honour, his research on cancer was inconclusive. Now that insulin had demonstrated its effectiveness, the clinical aspects had become routine, although each patient remained a special case. Naturally, in his heart of hearts, Fred had to be jealous of Bert's dizzying advances in the field of hormones. Fred had met Hans at the convention. They had said little, but Fred had immediately recognised all the qualities that would make the young doctor an excellent researcher.

Fred's difficult and taciturn character had caused him to separate from Marion, despite their little son Bill. Marion was fond of everything Fred hated: cocktail parties, receptions and large social events. They had quickly become estranged. His constant travelling, his intense professional activity, and his fascination for painting and for the arts left little time for life as a couple. Their divorce had caused a stir because Fred was a Nobel laureate and a prominent personality, the kind reporters love. He had been knighted Sir Frederick Banting. He spoke very little of this in his letters, but I sensed increasing worry, anxiety of a different order, the fear of another war. No doubt his memories of the Front were resurfacing. He was anything but indifferent to what was happening in Europe, particularly in Germany.

The conference gave us the opportunity to meet again. Bert had the great honour of giving the plenary lecture on anti-hormones, the work that we had carried out together. To my surprise, Fred was there and was the first to congratulate Bert for his excellent presentation. I learned with astonishment that

Fred had invited Bert and me to dinner in the best restaurant in Toronto.

"And no tuxedos or ties! Dress is casual. And I warned them that we did not want to be disturbed under any circumstances. I'll see you at seven."

A charming woman, elegant, intelligent and very sensitive, accompanied Fred.

"Gentlemen, please meet my future wife, Henrietta Ball. Like all of us here, Henrietta is devoted to research, but in cancer. We met in the laboratory, and it seems that we're not the only ones! Her parents have a house in Stanstead, in southern Quebec, just across the US border."

Henrietta talked about her work at the hospital. She was anxious that the diseases grouped under the term cancer be treated more effectively so we would no longer see patients, both young and old, dying every day.

"Between the four of us, it looks as if we cover several fields of biomedical research," Fred said.

Now Bert spoke.

"Fred, I hope you know that McLeod died, in Scotland. He suffered a great deal from osteoarthritis after he left Toronto."

"I do not want to hear about it, not even his name."

"Listen, Fred, sorry, Sir Frederick, all that is past."

"If anyone here calls me Sir again, I'll punch him in the face. I had to accept that honour, and others, by the way. But what the hell do I care about their decorations? Can't they leave me alone? Come on, let's change the subject. How's life in Montreal?"

"As you saw, all is well," said Bert, having waited for Fred to calm down. "Things are running smoothly at the lab, although we need to think about giving genuine recognition to the work of the outstanding students we train. I should like to keep them all, but doctors find it more lucrative to enter the private sector. As for scientists, they have a miserable living. We have nothing to offer them, and if this continues, they'll leave and possibly go to other countries or give up research. As you know, our National Research Council, the NRC, only gives a few grants for physics and tuberculosis research. Fortunately we are in relatively wealthy universities, but what can be done in the rest of the country? I could never get help from the Rockefeller Foundation. Luckily, we have the insulin subsidies, a few patents and donors."

"I see your point," Fred replied. "Besides, I met one of your students, Hans Selye, I think. Brilliant young man!"

"He takes too many shortcuts for my liking, but he does have ideas. Whether they are good or not remains to be seen. What were we taking about? Ah yes, Montreal. Brain research has been more fortunate at McGill, the way bacteriology has been in other places. They have built a remarkable Neurological Institute, led by the neurosurgeon Wilder Penfield."

"Yes, I've met him. A remarkable man; very cultivated. He talked about paintings I didn't even know existed. Bert, what do you think the NRC can do?"

"As I said, increase funding for medical research. You know very well that's where the future lies. Working on health today doesn't only mean saving lives, but also helping Canadians to live better and longer. And someday, if we get a system of social protection like the one they are trying to establish in France, the state will have to spend less money because the population will be healthy."

"I take it you lean towards progressive ideas?"

"I don't want to interrupt the conversation, but I think Bert is right."

"I agree with Paul," said Henrietta. "Fred, you're the chairman for the Council's Committee for Medical Research... You have to fight and get what Bert and all of you are asking for."

As we talked, I recognised Fred's expression, the closed face he had when he was deep in thought, the particular attitude that was a prelude to an important decision, at least when he was not angry.

"Since you think this is the way forward, despite current difficulties and the dark years ahead, well, Bert, if you're in agreement, of course I will nominate you as an associate member of the Council. That way you can assert your opinions more easily. Unfortunately for you, Paul, it isn't possible: there are only Canadians in this instance."

"Never mind, I have enough of that kind of work as it is."

Fred did not want to continue on the subject. He was a master in the art of suddenly changing the course of a conversation.

"By the way, Paul, don't tell me a nice boy like you is still single?"

"Well I am and I'm not, it depends on your definition of 'single'."

"Researchers are incorrigible. Every word, every little turn of phrase starts a discussion."

"So you have a girlfriend?" Henrietta asked softly.

"Yes, she lives in Quebec. She teaches at Laval University."

"The university run by priests? Don't tell me they approve of you being with this girl without being married!"

"Please don't be so sarcastic, Fred," said Henrietta, growing angry.

"Actually, Fred, we haven't said anything to the parish priest yet. Besides, I think he'll be the last person to be told. I was raised in a secular environment, so if ever I were to get married, I don't think it would be in a church."

"In Quebec, you'll be hard put to do otherwise."

"Then we'll go somewhere else."

"I see you're still as combative as ever, Paul, and nothing daunts you. I told you, Henrietta, how Paul and I met, even before I met Bert."

The dinner lasted late into the night. We talked about all our years together, like true veterans. Upon leaving us, Fred told me he was about to start a new life with Henrietta, and asked,

"Your friend, what does she teach at Laval?"

"Nuclear physics."

~ *CHAPTER 30* ~

The next day I was invited to dinner at Charley and Margaret's. In recent years, they had left the first house they had bought in Toronto with the Nobel Prize money for a bigger one on Old Forest Hill Road. It was an imposing redbrick residence surrounded by a large garden. The vast living room was tastefully decorated with Margaret's special touch. There were magnificent paintings on the walls and photos of their many trips around the world. Upstairs were six bedrooms, also beautifully decorated, and three bathrooms that Margaret insisted on showing me so that I could describe the house to her friend Louise. On the top floor were the lodgings of Ms. Cook, who looked after the children. Sandy was already seven and we had seen him on a visit to Quebec with his parents. But I did not yet know Henry, who was four. Sandy wanted me to tell him about Australia before bedtime. Henry too had his turn, listening attentively to a kangaroo story I had invented.

We then moved to the table. I gazed at a small painting that hung in the dining room next to a pastel portrait of Margaret by one of her artist friends.

"Charley, I've seen that painting in a larger version, I think."

"You're right, Paul. I've started painting, as an amateur. That painting is a small reproduction of the church of St. Fidele. The original was done by Fred and is hanging in the lab."

"He has real talent, our colleague."

"He does, I agree, Paul... And you know what? I have brought back some very good wine from France. But since I've had my ulcer, I've stopped drinking and smoking, and I cannot eat spicy food either. Tonight, because my great friend is here, I'll drink just half a glass of white wine with you. I've become serious, you see. You told me one day that I had to learn to do that! And since my return from Henry Dale's in London, I've learned strict precision in work and new ways of thinking and analysing results. I've become a true researcher, you know. I took over as department director after McLeod left."

Charley continued to tell me about life in the laboratory.

"I'll tell you the truth, Paul. Fred didn't like it when I took over as director. Yet an institute had been created for him in the same building, just above our department! He immersed himself in cancer research. That's not an easy task, and I think he realises that he doesn't really have the soul of a researcher. He has not surrounded himself with the sort of high-calibre, keen young scientists that make a laboratory's success. He is angry with me, I don't know why. With all his honours, he could very well keep on at the clinic and gain a little perspective. Besides, he travels a lot between Washington and Ottawa where, as you know, he works with the NRC, and all across Canada, not to speak of his forays to Europe. He always takes his brushes and canvases. Fun for a researcher, right?"

"Yes, I know all that. We had dinner together with Bert last night."

"Well, well! He's reconciled with Bert and continues to snub me?"

"You know, distance can be beneficial."

"Did he say anything about me?"

"No, Mr. Egocentric. We didn't talk about you."

"At least nobody is angry with you. How do you manage that? How is it possible in this business not to be on bad terms with anyone?"

"It comes with age. Try not to show off too much. How's the research going?"

"Fine, but I don't want to think about insulin. I've had enough. Though, thanks to insulin, I live well, as you can see. We've started to research those anticoagulant molecules that may block thrombotic phenomena. Heparin is a great discovery that has just been approved for use in blood transfusions. It's a sort of follow-up to the work I did at Dale's in London on blood pressure and the discovery of choline and histamine."

Margaret had prepared a delicious supper.

"My poor Margaret, how tired you must be of hearing us talk science. Tell me about yourself. How are you? The boys are wonderful. And did you enjoy your stay in Old Europe?"

"It's been quite a long time since we got back to Toronto, Paul – ten years. But our stay in Europe was extraordinary. London is a very exciting city. We discovered all kinds of treasures. Here we don't have museums or historical sites as interesting as the ones they have in England. I loved London."

"It's true," said Charley. "And what's more, she often came home later than me. I used to wonder where she was."

"That's enough, Charley. As you can see, Paul, my husband is jealous... You got our letters; you know we took the opportunity to visit several countries. We were received everywhere with full honours. Just think of it, Charley Best, co-discoverer of insulin! Mr. Professor is known throughout Europe, did you know that? Naturally we went to Paris. A wonderful city, probably the most beautiful in the world."

"Yes, I know, and I was very jealous. I have never been there. Maybe one day..."

"If you are going with Louise, I'll give you the address of the Hôtel de Malte, where we stayed. A very good location, near the *Bibliothèque Nationale*. You'll spend beautiful nights there. French theatre is a dream. We went to see Cyrano de Bergerac. A real jewel, even if my charming husband didn't understand everything. And what about you? How are you getting along? Things seem to be going well with Louise."

"There is nothing you can hide from women, they just guess!"

"Well... We write and often chat on the phone."

"And of course she only says bad things about me?"

"You men always think we're only interested in you! She would prefer you to be with her in Quebec for sure, but... work comes first."

"It's not easy just seeing each other on weekends, and not every week, come to that. But at least by passing only a few days together, we're less likely to grow tired of each other."

"She is doing such exciting things. Radioactivity, nuclear power, as she puts it."

"I don't understand much of it, but it's true that it sounds exciting."

"You don't plan to get married?"

"What is this, an epidemic? I was asked the same question yesterday."

"Well, it's not as if you are still twenty..."

Bla, bla, bla...

It was late, I took my leave. I had to get up early the next day to return to Montreal.

"The next time you come to Toronto, we'll play golf."

"You know I don't play golf."

"Well, then you'll have to learn."

~ *CHAPTER 31* ~

I made use of a subterfuge to avoid having Bert drive me home. I pretended to have an errand to do near the station. I thought of Hans, who did not speed. Athletic, he would cycle from place to place in Montreal, in all kinds of weather. When he arrived at the lab, he climbed the stairs, sometimes with his bicycle on his back. In his new department, he was given a large office, as well as space to work. He quickly adopted what he liked about Bert's lab: open meetings with students, the chairs placed in a half-circle around him to discuss research protocols, the ritual bell at around 10:30 in the morning and 3:00 in the afternoon to signal break time with hot drinks and biscuits. The sacrosanct daily visit to the autopsy room to discuss results. At weekends, I invited myself to the ceremonial, though I didn't belong to the department. In his office Hans had a well-stocked bar of various alcoholic beverages, especially Hungarian wines, like the Tokaj he continued to have brought in, heaven knows how, from his country.

"The bar is open!" he announced every Friday afternoon.

Students who entered his laboratory for the first time were a little disconcerted. Hans had remained faithful to certain

European traditions that were unknown to young Canadians. He showed them old-fashioned signs of respect. He called young women students *'Mademoiselle'*, and he had organised separate offices for men and women. Communication was carried out through a microphone by a secretary who called people by their first and last names. All this amused me. It made me think that if one day Hans were to head a large institute, it would be clearly distinct from any establishment to be found on the North American continent. And maybe that was just as well.

We often chose to meet at the Café de Paris, in the Ritz Hotel on Sherbrooke Street. He liked the place, which reminded him of his last year in Paris. And it made me feel as if I were in France. Paris never ceased to haunt me. I would have liked to go to the international exhibition but I had too much work to do. Hans spoke of his time there, and then about the more distant past, in Hungary. One could sense in him a wound that had not healed. One day he asked me,

"What did your father think when you told him you were choosing research and not a medical career? For mine, it was unthinkable. He had a clinic in Czechoslovakia. He wanted me to be a surgeon, like him. When I insisted on doing research, he said, 'is this what you want to do for your whole life? Play at watching the waves come in, like a child?' Did I ever tell you how I learned to speak several languages? Nine in all."

"Nine? I'm impressed! I can barely master English and French. In Canada, we're all immigrants. Everyone knows at least two languages."

"With a Hungarian father, a Viennese mother, and a French governess, I had to deal with three languages almost from the day I was born. I lived in Czechoslovakia. I had to learn

Russian and Polish. And then I studied Latin and Spanish in the seminary, a year in Rome, a year in Paris, six months in Baltimore… that's why I'm a polyglot!"

"That's great. It helps you expand your publication credits. If I were you, I would write the same thing in each language and publish it in a local journal."

"Are you kidding?"

"Not really. You published the hypophysectomy technique in German. Which really upset Evans by the way."

And so, by spending time with Hans, I learned to appreciate Tokaj, of which he seemed to have an inexhaustible supply. We would drink and chat. I felt very close to European culture. Hans did not discuss his private life. He preferred to talk about research. I knew he was married to Pina, the daughter of a wealthy American industrialist. That was probably how he could afford to live next to the university. I asked him no questions and he asked none of me. Our main headquarters was the Café de Paris, and that suited both of us.

As for Fred, he wrote me and sent me news of Europe. Disturbing news. Back from London, in that winter of 1938, he said that a new war was likely to break out. The rise of Nazism in Germany, the annexation of Austria and the Sudetenland, anti-Semitic measures and attacks against intellectuals were now our main concerns. Hans thought of his parents, who had remained in Czechoslovakia. His father was Jewish. Charley, meanwhile, had received numerous letters from scientists wanting to immigrate to Toronto. Sir Henry Dale, his mentor in England, helped him in this initiative. Bert, now part of the NRC, was not optimistic.

"Paul," said Bert, "I have just come back from Ottawa. I'll tell you a secret. We were asked to think about what biology and medicine could contribute in case of a conflict involving

Canada, but also other countries associated with the British Empire. I'm afraid they may ask us to change our research areas rather quickly to focus on those specific areas of research."

"You know, Bert, it is possible to reorient our work without deviating from research in endocrinology."

"So, do you mean you have an idea in mind?"

"When you're a researcher, you always have an idea in mind."

That simple statement got me pulled in a new war. But I only understood that later.

~ *CHAPTER 32* ~

I had just received an official letter from the NRC asking me to sit on the committee on biomedical research. It was easy enough to know where that decision originated.

I waited for Bert in the lab Monday morning. The screech of tyres announced his arrival.

"Bert, what's this letter I just received from the NRC?"

"All scientists are liable to be asked to take part in the war effort."

"But I'm not Canadian, as Fred so kindly pointed out last time in Toronto."

"But you are a citizen of the British Empire, so..."

"I am Australian. That isn't the same thing."

"Yes it is."

I felt it was useless to argue the point.

"So is it you I have to thank for the honour of being invited to sit on this committee?"

"Thank Fred, he's the President."

"And how am I supposed to help?"

"You told me you had ideas. All ideas, even the most outlandish, are welcome in these difficult times."

For the first time, I was angry with Bert. I seized my coat to go out for a breath of air. I needed to think and to talk to someone.

Just at that moment, Hans arrived on his bicycle, much quieter than Bert in his backfiring car.

"You look a little under the weather."

"I need to talk to you. Not here. Let's go to our meeting place."

"It must be important."

"Yes, it is."

The Café de Paris was always very quiet in the morning. I led Hans to a table in the back.

"What are you afraid of? Spies?"

"A little. I won't beat about the bush. You're my friend, Hans; I can trust you, can't I?"

"What a question!"

"Look, I got a letter asking me to be on the NRC biomedical research committee."

"Congratulations, Monsieur Dormont. What an honour!"

"Stop it, Hans, this is serious. It would be fine if I had not also been asked to think about the possible use of research as a weapon of war. You heard me: a weapon of war. They're asking me, who served in that terrible war of '14 to '18! I saw the disasters caused by gases and deadly weapons, and now I'm being asked to think up a weapon of war based on research!"

"And of course Dr. Banting and Bert are behind this."

"It truly surprises me from Fred. He saw trench warfare too!"

"Maybe it's just a study committee."

"This means that all laboratories, including yours, will also have to be involved."

"You don't really think that, do you?"

"Unfortunately, I do. So, let's try to calm down and quietly put our heads together. The articles you just wrote on the pervasive alarm reaction in animals after the administration of toxic agents, or even in situations of discomfort, don't you think people will see those as an original source of information?"

"You must be joking! Bert doesn't believe in my theory. You know that's why I left. I followed your advice: I continued to give him my help as an anatomist when he needed it."

"I know, and I appreciate it. But I've always believed your theory was right, otherwise we wouldn't have kept working together."

"You're not Bert."

"But now I'm on the same committee!"

"You're getting on my nerves! You know that we can't force a research topic on ourselves. I'm trying to elucidate something that will revolutionize the world of biology. Do you think I have time to worry about what people in Ottawa decide?"

"Hans, you know as well as I do what's happening in Europe, especially in your country. For intellectuals like us... like your parents."

There was a long silence.

"If I can help, I will," Hans replied.

"That's what I was hoping."

This situation brought us even closer. We decided not to meet in public places like the Café de Paris, except to talk about unimportant things. Now we would meet in his office, where he displayed a portrait of Claude Bernard, one of Biedl, his master in Europe, and another of Einstein, signed. There was also a large world map dotted with little flags representing the countries where his students and visitors came from.

"You know that, despite Bert's criticism, that article is starting to be quoted on a regular basis… the one in *Nature* on the observations after administration of various agents that produce a decrease in thymus weight, ulcers and adrenal retraction. I call it a non-specific syndrome, the alarm reaction in the body. I don't like the term, and one day I'll have to find another. Well, I'm sure that if put in a difficult position, all of us would have the same type of response."

"In our profession, you don't really think we have atrophied glands?"

"No, because, if your body reacts well, the symptoms do not appear."

"I've heard that. My father talked to me about the work of Claude Bernard, who described the importance of maintaining the internal environment, as the great physiologist called it."

"Right, like Walter Cannon, who more recently called it 'homeostasis'."

"So your thing would be a disruption of homeostasis?"

"Yes, in a way," Hans replied, thinking.

"Then, a soldier in war is in a situation of disrupted homeostasis. And on the other hand, it's conceivable to boost one's own defence capabilities to confront the enemy."

"I see where you're headed. We'll talk about it later."

~ *CHAPTER 33* ~

My work on anti-hormones was slowly advancing. But did these anti-hormones really exist? With the methods we had, it was impossible to bring them to light in the blood. Hans, never short of arguments that often combined philosophy and science, helped me reflect on my own work.

"Don't confuse the importance of your goal or the refinement of your instruments with the meaning of your work. Search for techniques that adapt to your problem and not for problems that adapt to techniques."

"But, Hans, what if we're headed straight for a dead end? You publish with us, what do you think?"

"Fight fiercely for what you believe, 'tis a noble goal, but abandon all effort when you know you're beaten'."

"You get on my nerves with all your quotes, Hans."

"Those aren't quotes, they're inspiration."

"And what does your inspiration suggest?"

"Can we think about this in another way? When a hormone is injected several times, there is often a resistance phenomenon. The hormone is unresponsive. Do we fully agree? Bert likened it to an immunological problem. Our immune system responds by creating antibodies, as if we were introducing a foreign substance. Do you still agree, Paul?"

"Yes of course. Anyway, Mac, my Australian friend, told me about it."

"I don't know Mac, but this is what we know right now about the basic principles of immunology. But we cannot find these antibodies. So we need to think of something else. I have often thought about it. What if the resistance didn't affect the substance itself, but the place where it is active?"

"Oh, yes… Where are you going with this, Hans?"

"The administered substance has to be recognised by an entity located on the unit it acts upon. Take the adrenal hormones for example. They could recognise the gland itself, regulating the homeostasis, or like a true hormone, go to another organ, such as the liver, on which hormones are known to provide energy."

"So you mean that, rather than in the blood, it is on the organ itself that we should be looking?"

"I think so."

"What a great idea!"

"Don't get excited, Paul. It's only a theory: just as far-fetched as the one Bert refuses to believe in."

I did not get a wink of sleep that night. What was he talking about? It was like searching for a needle in a haystack. How could the things we were doing possibly answer that question?"

Bert noticed I was tormented.

"Were you out celebrating last night? Your hair is a rat's nest. Did Louise arrive unannounced?"

"Stop, it has nothing to do with Louise. Yesterday I had a long scientific discussion with Hans."

"And he convinced you to throw yourself, body and soul, into the physiology of incomprehensible mechanisms?"

"Not at all. We talked about anti-hormones. I think we're on the wrong track."

"I'm listening. If Hans has any new ideas, I'm interested."

I reported our exchange as accurately as possible. The more I explained the more attentive Bert grew.

"And what do you suggest?"

"To find molecules that could bind themselves to these cellular entities. This is a job for a biochemist, right? That way, we could consider blocking the effects of an injected substance, and thereby reproduce the resistance phenomenon we have all observed."

"It's a good idea."

"Especially as finding a molecule that could block a soldier's fear in battle and stimulate his aggressiveness, would then protect him against the shocks of war. And that would be a very good thing. Right?"

"I see that you're becoming interested in this committee."

The committee discussed different aspects of the potential involvement of biological approaches during conflict. To my great surprise, Fred had taken a passionate interest in the clothing needed by pilots in case of depressurisation and acceleration of gravity. He envisaged a special coverall filled with water. In a similar scientific perspective, others on the committee were interested in submarines and clothing or footwear adapted to different climatic conditions. The Toronto group met at the NRC. Charley had been appointed at the same time as me. Later, it was Hans's turn, not without resistance from some who were suspicious of this man from Eastern Europe. Charley had chosen to focus on the naval sector and research on motion sickness, specifically seasickness, for the troops. In his laboratory, he developed techniques for conserving dried blood. Bert and I were in charge of the problem of shocks linked to the activities of the adrenal glands and blood substitutes. Later, Hans joined us.

All debates in the committee centered on two main problems: biological weapons, and the funds required for the development of research. Fred managed to convince the government that without substantial financial support, it would be impossible for laboratories to follow our recommendations. For large universities in Ontario and Quebec, it was most important to persuade researchers of the need to change some of their policies. The carrot of financing proved an effective weapon. Unfortunately it was obvious that apart from those of Ontario and Quebec, Canada had too few university infrastructures able to compete with large American or European universities. To remedy the situation, a significant financial contribution would have to be made. The government quickly understood this. The budget of the NRC, and therefore of research, in this time of crisis, rapidly increased to levels never attained even in times of prosperity. It would open up jobs in the most poorly funded universities.

If the financial part was subject to a broad consensus in the committee, it was quite the opposite for biological weapons. We all agreed about developing remedies against infections or injuries of war, but the use of chemical or biological weapons was subject to debate.

On this matter, Fred had created a secret committee to determine ways of using microorganisms such as cholera, typhoid, anthrax and even gas. Several of us had spoken out against such proposals.

"British intelligence services have reported that for several months, German factories have been manufacturing poison gas, such as mustard gas. Several defectors from that country, recently arrived in the United States, confirmed this as well as the fact that chemical and pharmaceutical industry factories were also preparing bacteria capable of contaminating an entire army."

"Sir Frederick that is no reason for us to do the same. Do you think Canadians are ready to accept the consequences of such a war? How can we reasonably imagine that a provoked epidemic will attack only soldiers and remain within a limited area? This war will not be the same as that of 14-18. The days of trench warfare are past. This will be a moving war, as unfortunately we can see with the advance of the German panzers."

"I grant you it's a risk. And many of our American colleagues have expressed the same reluctance."

"Could we not find a compromise, like false information?"

"I don't understand," Fred replied to this question from a committee member.

"Through our intelligence service we could lead people to believe that we too are developing chemical and biological weapons, even more dangerous than those that currently exist. That way, we could hope for our opponents to give up. However, that doesn't stop us from working on other aspects, such as the development of products to deal with potential outbreaks or help improve the health of our troops."

"A sensible statement at last!" commented one of our colleagues.

"A few years ago, my friend Alexander Fleming gave me some strains of Penicillium notatum," said Charley. "We could ask Connaught, with whom we worked on insulin, to produce large quantities of penicillin."

"Dr. Selye suggests that we work on shock-prevention or battling fatigue with adrenal gland extracts."

"There are also sulphonamides for infections."

"Thank you, gentlemen," said Fred, "I see we have a lot of work ahead."

~ *CHAPTER 34* ~

Life can be full of surprises and disturbing coincidences. When I arrived home from Ottawa, a letter from Melbourne was waiting for me in the mailbox. My friend Mac had written to tell me he was coming to Montreal for a conference on viruses. I had not seen Mac for years. I rushed to the post office to send him a telegram that would reach him before he left Melbourne. I told him that I was expecting him and would be delighted to have him stay with me. Meanwhile Hans, whom I had talked to about Mac, said he would be hosting a Czech chemist colleague and acquaintance of his father who had once been a lecturer in Zagreb and now worked in Switzerland.

I was overjoyed to see Mac. He stayed with me for over a week. We talked late into the night. We had so much to tell each other after all these years. I almost felt homesick when he spoke of Melbourne, the heat and the sea. Mac had gone abroad as all of us had. He had worked on bacteriophages at the Lister Institute in London. In the laboratory he had met Edith, whom he had married. They had three children. Bacteriology and virology had evolved a great deal in recent years and what he said was exciting, for example, that bacteriophages could multiply with the host bacteria without the host actually becoming ill. He spoke of his work on viruses, including herpes, flu and Q fever. In his lab at Walter and Eliza Hall Institute, he had just developed a vaccine for Japanese river fever. The vaccine was tested in England. During one of our conversations, I asked him his opinion on the possible spread of viruses and bacteria. His answer was categorical. We had no antidote to block them, and that could result in disaster for humanity. His demonstration that of a true specialist, showed that we were right not to forge out in that direction. But the time flew by. Soon Mac was to return to Melbourne.

In the days following his departure, I had a sense of emptiness. I had not had time to introduce him to Louise, who had been detained in Quebec City. And then the discussion on anti-hormones started again with Hans. Bert was convinced that they were not antibodies in the immunological sense. You could see a resistance effect after repeated administrations of hormones but no substance to isolate. The idea of interaction between the bacteriophage and Mac's host bacteria came back to my mind.

"Tell me, Hans, what if the cell recognised our hormone and so, after a while, prevented it from acting?"

"That assertion has been made before, but how would you test it?"

As usual, Hans was right. I did not know how to go about it. In any case, his interest lay elsewhere, that is, in the body's reaction to attack. Not only had he regularly observed the effects of hypophysectomy on different organs, but he had also noticed that, conversely, when some of an animal's endocrine glands were removed, the pituitary gland itself showed histological changes. And finally, that the pituitary gland was probably somewhat controlled by the nerves. All this put him in a state of extreme excitement. He wanted to do everything, without delay.

One morning, when I dropped by his laboratory, he introduced me to the young Czech chemist he had told me about.

"Paul, I would like you to meet Vladimir Prelog. He is a chemist. You are sure to understand each other; biochemistry is partly chemistry, isn't it? I'll leave you to talk for a moment and if you like, Paul you could show him your laboratory."

Vladimir was a very composed young man. Even rather cold, I would say. Not very talkative. It seemed that was often the case with people from Eastern Europe.

"Is it the first time you've been to Canada?"

"Yes, we are not accustomed to travelling. Hans must be an exception. He seems to like living here."

"I think so. He is ambitious and he never runs out of ideas. I am sure he will be successful."

"Our parents know each other, that's why I contacted him."

"He told me. So you are a chemist?"

"I work in organic chemistry."

"What do you know about hormones?"

"Nothing, apart from what Hans just told me."

"Do you believe that a hormone is likely to attach itself to something that could destroy it?"

"Destroy it, I don't know. But prevent it from acting, yes, that is possible."

"How is it possible?"

"In chemistry, we imagine structures taking different forms. We can bind them to things similar to ghosts that will correspond exactly to the chemical structure."

"I don't follow you..."

"If you have a drawing board, I can show you."

Vladimir drew circles of different colours connected by bars and explained how molecules, and probably our hormones are made.

"Could this type of molecule be easily manufactured?"

"Easily, that depends, but at least we have a few bases like cyclic compounds, such as those I have drawn here. For we chemists, it is like a construction set. We put the carbons or hydrogens next to each other and check if it can work."

"I don't think we could do all that in chemistry."

"It's not just biology that invents, you know. For example, the recent discovery of adamantane, a product extracted from petroleum that releases a camphor odour. I try to make some because it looks like a diamond. A diamond is beautiful, but very complex. I wonder how this molecule is formed."

I spent the next night dreaming of flying molecules of every colour that constantly changed shape, as if reflected in distortion mirrors in a funhouse.

~ *CHAPTER 35* ~

Fred's sense of foreboding, and his growing pessimism that was particularly evident each time he returned from London, was unfortunately justified. In Germany, preparations for war had suddenly intensified. The armies of the Reich had invaded Poland, which had signed a military alliance agreement with Britain. Britain was at war, the Dominions too. Denmark, Norway, Belgium and the Netherlands were the next to be invaded. In France, it was a debacle. Nothing resisted the advance of the German troops. There were significant losses among the Anglo-French troops encircled in the pocket of Dunkirk.

Fred had been given instructions by the NRC. We had been ordered to conclude our work of reflection to increase the competitiveness of Canadian university research. Now all the laboratories needed to focus on work that was useful to the nation. This concerned all of us, whether physicists, chemists or biologists.

We at the laboratories of Toronto and Montreal were ready, because of the discussions at the NRC.

I had convinced the committee that our work on hormones could be part of biology's arsenal for the war effort. Perhaps they could serve as an antidote. Fred's lab had decided to work on mustard gas. One day he came limping into a meeting. Everyone noticed.

"Have you hurt yourself?"

"Sort of. I wanted to test an antidote for mustard gas. It burned my skin slightly. I'm not concerned about myself; I thought I'd treat the burns when I got home. But then I found the entire family in great turmoil. My son had set fire to some crates in the garden. It was windy. We had to extinguish the fire quickly. By the time I had repaired the damage, my burn had spread. Fortunately, Henrietta was there. She found compresses for me. Now what's on the agenda?"

Fred saw we were having trouble keeping straight faces.

"Laugh as much as you want, gentlemen! I almost lost my leg! Come on, show me your reports!"

"We have made good progress on penicillin production from the strains obtained from Fleming," said Charley. "We've arranged for people to donate blood so it can be dried and transported to areas of conflict. Meanwhile, Connaught Laboratories has managed to make some cortin from beef adrenals to mitigate the shocks experienced by soldiers. I have an Australian colleague who is working on a flu vaccine and another in England who is also preparing penicillin."

"I see that all our partners have got right down to work," Fred said.

"And what about our American colleagues?"

"They'll get to work when they see it's become necessary for them!"

"Right. Have these gentlemen from Montreal anything to say about their work?"

"The study of the body's adaptation to a new environment is entirely appropriate in wartime," reported Hans.

"Yes, but it remains basic research," said Bert.

"For now, perhaps, but I foresee many applications."

"We will discuss that at the next meeting. Thank you, gentlemen," said Fred, "I wish you a safe return to your respective laboratories."

I kept thinking back to my discussion with Vladimir Prelog. Montreal chemists had to be able to produce molecules that could prevent the action of hormones. If Hans's theory were true, if it were possible to block the adrenocorticotropic function of the pituitary gland, that of the ACTH hormone discovered by Bert, it could help soldiers adapt to the conditions of war.

The chemistry lab was on McGill campus. There were stills everywhere, strange smells, a mixture of alcohol, camphor, and ether, pleasant but sometimes unpleasant too. Like Vladimir, chemists also had montages of multicoloured balls on their desks.

"Does it amuse you to have objects like this everywhere? They look like pieces from Meccano sets."

"That's true, but every montage represents something important, a chemical molecule."

"Can you really represent biological molecules?"

"You can always try."

This is how the McGill chemistry laboratory started working on it. We spent several months mixing organic solvents, activating acids, protecting or de-protecting them by removing anything water-soluble, to end up with a product soluble in organic solvents.

"Paul, we still have an evaporation step to do and then we can give you a finished product."

I finally had something new in hand. A compact white

powder at the bottom of a glass tube. Did this product, straight out of a scientist's imagination, have any real utility? No one knew, at least, not me. It had to be tested.

It was better to carry out the experiments in Hans's laboratory. He had the animals, and he knew better than anyone how to observe them.

Lab rats made it easy for us to experiment. And yet, our early experiments were a disaster. The injections irreparably caused the animals' death. We could not go on like this.

By decreasing the dose, we managed to keep the animals alive. But either nothing happened or one could only observe toxic effects. The results were no better than those achieved with tissue extracts in earlier days.

To make headway in research, one must show great tenacity and have a lot of time: weeks, and sometimes months. We changed the protocols; we gained better mastery of the variables of administration. As acute injections in small doses did not have much effect, we decided to use chronic administrations. Some tissues were beginning to respond: decreased weight of the thymus and adrenal, some changes in the animal's behaviour.

"What if we put our animals in conditions of intense disturbance?" asked Hans.

"We're not taking the animals up to the roof and setting off the siren again, especially not in wartime. We'd go straight to prison. I can just see the headlines: 'Two leading researchers from McGill University, members of the NRC, distinguish themselves with reckless med student pranks'."

Hans burst into contagious laughter that relaxed the atmosphere a little.

~ *CHAPTER 36* ~

We had to be serious and perform our experiments inside the laboratory. Hans had noticed that laboratory rats did not like to be alone and began endlessly exploring when put in a different cage. He had already observed that humans sometimes behaved the same way in this type of situation. Their behaviour differed depending on whether they were alone or in company. Humans too looked all around when in a new environment.

Hans himself was looking around. He was looking for a new house. Several weeks before, he had spotted one next to McGill on Milton Street. He had heard it would soon be for sale, but he doubted the transaction could be made in wartime. He drew a parallel between himself, visiting houses, and the rat in front of him, looking around in the same way, sniffing, walking in circles inside his cage. I too was struck by the analogy.

"Your rat is behaving strangely. It looks disturbed, a little distressed. Obviously not very happy."

"It's funny you should say that, Paul, but I'm thinking exactly the same thing. If all the comments I've made on this general alarm reaction correspond to our situation when attacked, our bodies do indeed react appropriately. What do you think?"

"This theory holds, but it still needs to be demonstrated."

"You don't believe in my theories either, just like Bert!"

"If I didn't trust you, I wouldn't come to see you with my product."

"Paul, you were talking before about disturbance, distress... If we called it 'stress', that would sound good, wouldn't it? In addition, the word *stress* sounds like a snake hiss, easy to pronounce both in English and French. As in Racine... you know your classics! Remember what Oreste says in *Andromaque*: '*Pour qui sont ces serpents qui sifflent sur vos têtes?*'[3]. Well, Paul, shall we adopt the word 'stress'?"

"It's up to you. Moreover, to describe an unenviable situation, a word ending with the two letters of mad Hitler's Nazi group is a good illustration of your theory."

"So I'll adopt it. From now on, we will speak of stress. Life stress, the stress of war, Bert stresses me, my wife stresses me..."

We went on joking all the way to his office.

"Hans, what are we going to do with my product?"

"Are you stressed?"

"Indeed!"

"Very well. Let's put the animals under conditions of stress. We begin with morphological observations, and then move on to physiological measurements such as glucose, ketone bodies and corticosteroids released by the adrenal glands. What do you think? Then we can test your product on variables that have changed."

"I like the idea."

That is how, after months of work, Hans was eventually

---

[3]For whom are these snakes hissing on your heads?

able to confirm his theory of adaptation to a new environment, develop the idea that the stress axis plays a key role in the alarm reaction, as in the nervous system and the peripheral nerves, and finally that the adrenocorticotropic hormone, ACTH, discovered by Bert in the pituitary gland, was to play a fundamental role in the stress response.

My product proved just as effective in laboratory tests aimed at studying this stress axis. But the compound remained difficult to use because it was not very soluble and did not easily penetrate the tissues.

We were confident, sure that our research would be successful. But we still had to convince our colleagues at the NRC that our findings could contribute to the war effort. Hans had the gift of persuasion, self-assured sometimes to the point of arrogance. But he was thorough and the results were there. Research on the shocks received by soldiers was a priority. A single committee meeting, chaired by Fred, was enough to win acceptance for the idea of continuing the research, which opened up great prospects.

Consequently, Fred came to Montreal more often to keep track of our work and Bert's. Besides, Fred and Bert had become friends; their relationship had changed. And now, during his stay in Montreal, there was no question of Committee Chairman Sir Frederick staying anywhere but in Westmount with the Collips. Fred knew Bert's whole family, his wife Ray and their two daughters, down to their youngest child Jack. He could not escape games of pool in the special billiards room in the basement. He did not talk about it, but we knew he lost every time because Bert was an expert pool player. Fred also refrained from comment on Bert's sporty driving in the streets of Montreal.

It was February 1941. Fred had to go to London again to meet with the head of the Medical Research Centre and the President of the Royal Society, Sir Henry Dale, to discuss biomedical advances in both countries, and the as-yet passive attitude of the Americans. Naturally this mission was more risky than the previous ones because we were at war. Fred chose to fly rather than go by ship. Travelling in the Atlantic was anything but safe, due to constant attacks by German U-Boats.

Fred took the train to Toronto. He had to stop in Montreal for one night before heading to Newfoundland, where he would board a plane for England. He naturally asked Bert to put him up. He wanted to give Bert and Ray one of his latest paintings.

"As always, Ray, the meal was a delight. You really are a fabulous cook. I learned that your daughter Barbara had joined the army and worked in the laboratory?"

"She's been coming to the lab since she was a child. I prefer to see her work here instead of heaven-knows-where with our military. Let's go into the lounge. May I offer you some tobacco for your pipe?"

"No, thanks. I have my own, preciously stored in my little box, as usual, and slightly damp. It keeps better that way. I changed tobacco recently. Would you like to try it?"

"With pleasure."

"How are Bill and Henrietta?" Ray asked.

"Henrietta is very devoted to her work on cancer. I am sure she will become an excellent oncologist. We took a vacation this past summer at her parent's beautiful house in Stanstead, Quebec. Bill quite enjoyed it. It's very pleasant and relaxing. Very amusing too, being in a town that sits on the border of two countries. You never know if you're in Canada or in the United States."

"It's kind of the same thing in Toronto, isn't it?"

"That's true, but there is Lake Ontario. It is so big that you cannot see the other side. Like Canada facing Europe. There's just the Atlantic between us. Ah, poor Europe! The troops of the Reich have completely invaded it. They have sent an expeditionary force to Africa, from what I have been told."

"Hitler is another Napoleon, and even worse. I hope that the Allies will put an end to his progress before he proclaims himself emperor. One last game of pool, Fred?"

"I am a little tired, and tomorrow I have an early flight to Gander."

"Tomorrow I'll take you to the airport. Tell me, are you wearing your new water -pressurised suit to fly? You'll be able to test the effects of gravity."

"Unfortunately not, you know that bombers are not very fast and don't fly very high."

~ *CHAPTER 37* ~

On the way to the military airport, Fred started to talk. He especially wanted to avoid looking at the road.

"I really have too much work with the NRC presidency. It is Charley who should have gone to London to meet with his friend Sir Henry Dale and discuss the joint strategy to adopt with the Medical Research Centre. But it seems that Mr. Best is too busy with the project I asked him to coordinate, obtaining blood for the army. Did you know that Charley is rising ever higher in the ranks at the University of Toronto? He took advantage of my institute's not being directly linked to the university, and of the fact that I am a doctor and don't have much to do with the academic system, to pontificate at leisure. I hear a lot about him. When I think that one day that bastard Best will be given the Chair!"

"You can't keep lashing out at people, Fred. You snubbed me for years, and now we're friends. And now you go on about Charley when you praised him for years. He's younger than all of us. It would be perfectly normal for him to take your place one day. And do you think for me it's any better with Hans? Stop getting upset for nothing. Stop stressing, as the expression goes. You perhaps do not know, but those two young people are doing remarkable things. They are helping European researchers and their families to escape from Nazi barbarism. So, Mr. Chairman, let's put an end to these grievances."

Fred did not say another word for the entire trip.

The flight from Montreal to Gander proceeded normally. However, a big snowstorm was announced in Newfoundland for the following days. Therefore there was no possible way of taking off for England. The two barracks of the small Gander airport were pretty well insulated. Fred took the opportunity to write a story about the discovery of insulin and to do some painting. The five Hudson III T-9449 bombers stood side-by-side, neatly aligned on the tarmac. Every day, men were out busily shovelling snow and removing ice to prevent its accumulation on the wings. Finally, on the fifth day, the snow stopped falling. Captain Joseph Mackey informed his crew, Officer William Bird and operator William Snailham that they could finally take off.

That night of February 20, 1941, after the usual checks, the five planes took off one after the other with a deafening roar. The temperature was -20 ° C. Captain Mackey was a veteran pilot and perfectly mastered his plane. However, about an hour after takeoff, Fred sensed he was worried.

"Commander Mackey, is there a problem?"

"Something's not right with one of the engines. But don't worry, Sir Frederick, we checked everything before leaving."

He watched the temperature of the motors. It was climbing dangerously. Suddenly the left engine exploded. Mackey made the only reasonable decision: to return to Gander. He addressed his aircraft officer,

"Bill, alert NFL and request a QDM. Holding altitude at 5000 feet. Ask Sir Banting to come to the cockpit."

"Sir Frederick, we have a problem and we're going back to Gander. Take this parachute in case you need it."

Next, the right engine malfunctioned. The bomber had lost 2500 feet, but at least it was no longer over the ocean. Mackey opened the fuel valves to prevent the plane from exploding during the emergency landing. They could no longer see anything. The glass of the cockpit was covered with oil. A crash was inevitable. A wing hit an object in the dark, probably a tree. Then… nothing. Silence, darkness.

Long minutes passed without a sound. Then there was a stirring in the damaged cabin. Captain Mackey's head was throbbing. He had definitely hit something when landing. He had not had his seatbelt on so was thrown to the back of the plane. Fortunately, he could move, but his leg was atrociously painful.

"Bird, Snailham, Sir Frederick, answer me!"

Silence. Staggering forward through the cabin, he saw that his two companions were dead. They hadn't been able to use their parachutes.

"Oh, my God! How awful!"

He could not find Fred.

"Sir Frederick, answer me! Where are you?"

A groan was heard near the cockpit.

"Sir Frederick, do you hear me?"

Fred was bleeding profusely from the head. He complained of pain in his arm and his ribs. He uttered incomprehensible words, and incoherent sentences. Mackey ripped off a piece of parachute to serve as a compress for the open head wound. Fred kept talking nonsense.

"Ah, Doctor, thank you. I've never seen you before in the hospital, but you have a good head on your shoulders. You know what to do. Tell your assistant to administer more insulin to Mr. Smith. He's not very well at the moment. Tell him I'll see him tonight when I have finished my rounds. It's too hot in here. I need to open the door and get out."

Dr. Banting was delirious.

"Can you take notes? I have some information for Dr. Collip in Montreal. And tonight, I'm going to the theatre with Henrietta. Can you tell her I'll be late?"

"Of course."

Despite his own pain, Captain Mackey tried to keep Fred awake. Like any good pilot, he knew basic first aid. But Fred had fallen asleep. Mackey covered him with the parachute and two heavy coats so that he would not get a chill. Nothing worked in the plane. He knew he had to find assistance as soon as possible. If not, one of the greatest scientists ever was going to die.

Walking through deep snow without seeing where you are going, at night, in the cold, is an impossible task. After two miles, without having seen a living soul, he decided to turn back. When he approached the bomber, he saw that Fred was gone.

"Sir Frederick, where are you?"

Not a sound. The cockpit door hung open. Dr. Banting must have slipped out of the cabin. The first rays of sun appeared on the horizon. Captain Mackey realised that he had a bandage on his head. He did not remember applying it himself. Dr. Banting had probably saved his life in a moment of lucidity. He pondered this as he trudged through silent snow, following footprints that led to a thicket of trees. There he found Fred, Sir Frederick Banting, Nobel Prize for Medicine, leaning against a tree... dead.

~ *CHAPTER 38* ~

An alert was sent out when contact with the bomber was lost. But the visibility was so poor that it was impossible to locate the wreckage. It took two whole days for the fog to dissipate and for a reconnaissance aircraft to locate the plane. Captain Mackey had posted himself on top of a small hill to be easily spotted. The reconnaissance plane shot him a message as it passed overhead, "Sending reinforcements, hang tight."

Despite his injuries, Mackey had held up. There was enough food in the plane to ensure one man's survival for a week. After a few hours, he was rescued.

The news of Sir Frederick Banting's death spread like wildfire. All the newspapers changed their front page to carry the story. There was consternation all over Canada, particularly in Toronto, Montreal and Ottawa. Parliament suspended its session and the Prime Minister cancelled all meetings.

All the learned societies and the Nobel Committee prepared a tribute to the man who had saved so many lives.

Rumours of sabotage were becoming increasingly pointed. Counter-espionage specialists from Canada and the US, as well as experts from Lockheed, where the bombers had been built, were already at the site. How to explain that one of the devices had so seriously malfunctioned and that both engines had broken down? It was the only bomber carrying a passenger. And not just any passenger but an important public figure, head of a committee mandated to reflect on biological warfare, improvements in combat aircraft and the health of their pilots.

The inspection was conducted smoothly. Sand was found mixed with the fuel. The experts were categorical: it is always possible to take off safely in these conditions, but sand can block the flow of fuel and increase the engine temperature after about an hour of flight. That is precisely what had happened.

All the persons who were likely to have approached the bomber were interviewed, even the crew of the other four aircraft, which had arrived safely in England. It was time to face facts: the crash was the result of sabotage, no doubt perpetrated by the German intelligence service.

The body of Sir Frederick Banting was brought back to Toronto. A procession, followed by a huge crowd, left the university for the Mount Pleasant Cemetery where military honours were rendered. Several moving tributes from his colleagues, including Bert, who could barely contain his grief, referred to the greatest disaster to have ever occurred in the history of science in Canada. According to William Hall, the world would have to wait a long time to replace such a scientist. Political personalities filed by the coffin, which was carried by four men, including Charley Best, and lowered into the grave.

Henrietta, now Lady Banting, had enjoyed too short a married life with Fred. But she had friends. Charley and Margaret often visited her. Still, she was alone in her life as a woman and as an oncologist. Would life also change in the

Toronto and Montreal laboratories? Nothing would be the same as before.

Charley was now in charge of both his own laboratory and Fred's Institute. He was the last person that Fred would have wanted as a successor! But it was Bert who was called to take on Fred's most thankless burden: the chair of the NRC medical committee.

Despite the war escalating in Europe and budget cuts for everything unrelated to armaments, McGill University had decided to build an endocrinology institute for Bert in the western part of the medical faculty. For Hans, this meant that sooner or later he would have to leave McGill if he wanted his own endocrinology lab.

All these events had greatly upset me. Louise had joined me for Fred's funeral. Bert had talked with her for a long time, especially about her research in nuclear physics. She told me that she too had to go to London soon.

"But it's very dangerous. You saw what happened to Fred."

"I'm not a Nobel, well, not yet..."

"Stop making fun of me, will you."

"Nuclear physics is the science of the future. You never know..."

"Still, I am not going to run after you all my life. Quebec, Stockholm and now London!"

"But you're a frequent traveller, my love. I'll wait for you in London too, as I have done here and elsewhere."

Bert proved a skilled director of the NRC Committee. He was already looking ahead to after the war, when research in Canada would have to be reconstructed, the number of Canadian universities increased, the necessary funds found, scholarships offered to students to help them study medicine or science, and partnerships between universities and businesses developed. Bert had always liked setting goals, unlike Fred.

Hans and I had resumed our work on anti-hormones. But the product was still very soluble and sometimes slightly toxic.

"Tell me, Hans, your friend Vladimir, the chemist you introduced to me just before the war, does he still work in Switzerland?"

"I have not heard from him recently, but I learned that he had definitely left Czechoslovakia to take refuge in Switzerland. In Zurich, I believe, at the Federal Institute of Technology. I can find out if you want?"

McGill chemists were unable to help me. I had to try elsewhere. I told Bert about my concerns.

"Look, Bert, I'm sure I have a product that can block the stress response. It is very important for our soldiers, if it works on humans. I now know the chemical structure of the molecule thanks to the McGill chemists, but it still needs to be improved to achieve better tissue penetration. Some time ago, I met a friend of Hans, a top-notch chemist. He is now a refugee in Switzerland. I have to see him again."

"Do you realise what you're asking for? Going to Switzerland today is almost impossible. The Germans are occupying France; the French government is in Hitler's boot. People are constantly arrested and questioned. How can you imagine that you, a British citizen, could make your way to Switzerland? What do you think? It's far too dangerous!"

"May I remind you that I speak perfect French, which is an asset? I am just asking you to look around and see if we could do something. As you know, if we have control of an anti-stress compound, our persuasiveness in biological warfare against the Germans will be decisive."

~ *PART FOUR* ~

~ *CHAPTER 39* ~

I continued my research at McGill and remained concerned about the bad news from Europe. London was being constantly bombed. The Battle of Britain was raging but the English held firm. To deal with the situation, new pilots had to be trained and the production of aircraft and radars increased. It was an area in which Canada possessed considerable expertise.

The war had been raging for over a year and now civilians across Europe, women and children, were dying as well as soldiers. The Americans were still not ready to intervene. They would have been able to provide valuable logistical support, and it was too bad they would not mobilise. Within the NRC, our discussions about our American colleagues were of this order.

But everything changed at the end of 1941. On December 7, the Japanese, in the port of Pearl Harbour, attacked the US Navy, and many ships were destroyed. This sudden, violent attack called for a reaction. The US counter-attacked. In the Pacific, they needed the help of Australians and New Zealanders. In Europe, they had to support the British. For months, Churchill had attempted to persuade the Americans to take part in the fight but the American public remained largely hostile to any intervention. Now the deal had suddenly changed.

Our meetings at the NRC had become more frequent, which somewhat slowed our research. Hans and I had firmly refused Bert's offer to drive us to Ottawa for meetings. We did not want to risk our lives on the road, especially with winter and slippery roads ahead, for Bert could not resist the pleasure of showing off his driving prowess. The train was slower but far preferable. It gave us the opportunity to talk peacefully. We took advantage of this time to take stock of our experiments. The theories on the stress response had evolved into certainties. Stress also provided evidence that our body always adapted to assault in a most efficient manner, brilliantly illustrating Claude Bernard's ideas about the balance of the internal environment and Walter Cannon's on homeostasis.

At the end of one of these meetings in Ottawa, Bert took me by the arm and led me into a small adjoining room.

"Paul, do you still have that crazy idea of wanting to go to Switzerland?"

"You know very well I've barely made any progress on the compound's solubility and we are still observing toxic effects."

"So you still want to meet your chemist in Zurich? Are you sure there is no one any closer?"

"I don't think so. When I met him, he told me he could graft any molecule with a compound that allows for better tissue penetration."

"And you didn't ask what that compound consisted of?"

"Do you think he would have told me? He just talked about his research on a product extracted from oil."

"And do you think that he will reveal it to you now?"

"It is a risk that has to be taken. I'm sure it is worth the effort."

"I'm not so sure," Bert replied, "but since you are stubborn and I knew I wouldn't be able to dissuade you, I talked to someone who can help you get to Switzerland."

"Thanks..."

"He's a Canadian based in Washington, but he sometimes comes home. I asked him to let me know the next time he's here."

It was not long. A week later, William Stephenson was in Montreal. I explained why I wanted to go to Zurich. He listened carefully. His face showed no emotion.

"Your story is compelling, but I wonder if the passion for research deserves such sacrifice. You obviously think so, but the risks are enormous. I can help you go to Switzerland, but you are putting your life at risk and perhaps others' lives too."

"I am fully aware of that. And I expect you have been told about me. The Great War, my commitment to General Monash, my military medal, and of course, my participation in the NRC, though I'm Australian?"

"I know all that. That's why I trust you, but I still have to remind you of the risks of such a mission. You will have to contact people you know nothing about, who will tell you nothing but the bare necessities. It isn't easy to get to London these days, let alone Switzerland. You have to cross enemy lines. We will provide papers with a new identity and all the necessary documents. I wish you luck."

There were five passengers, including myself, in the military plane that had just left Montreal to cross the Atlantic. For security reasons, we were told that we would land in Manchester rather than London. I had to stop thinking about

Fred's accident. I could not swallow anything. Nobody said a word. Besides, the engine noise made it difficult to engage in even the slightest exchange. I finally fell asleep and slept until dawn. When I opened my eyes, we were about to land.

~ *CHAPTER 40* ~

The closer we got to London, the more apocalyptic the landscape became. Crumbling buildings, and black smoke rising in the dark sky. The nightmare of the trenches came back to me and hit me hard. I had relegated those terrible images of war to the depths of my memory. A car was waiting at Victoria Station, which, fortunately, had been spared. The car moved with difficulty around the heaps of rubble. I would have liked to see London differently, in all its splendour and graceful evenings. This was nothing of the sort, only darkness and melancholy.

I had not heard from Louise for a long time. It is true that mail travelled slowly, especially when it was not priority mail for military staff. At least that is what I told myself for reassurance. I just hoped she had not changed address since the beginning of her stay in London.

The car dropped us off in the centre of town, on Baker Street. It was fun to see the street name, so familiar from the adventures of Sherlock Holmes. He had been the hero of a war correspondent Monash had met in France. On the door of the old Victorian building was a plaque that read: SOE: *Special Operations Executive*. Each of the five passengers was received separately.

"Hello, Mr. Dormont, you're probably wondering what you're doing here?"

"Indeed I am."

"We are responsible for helping you get to Switzerland to meet your colleague. We took the precaution of collecting some information about him. It's Vladimir Proleg, isn't it?"

"Yes."

"At first we feared he might be a Nazi agent. We must be extremely vigilant about people who have lived in the East, even if they have left their country. I assure you, he isn't an agent. But the passage to Switzerland is not easy. We cannot parachute you in at the moment, it would be too risky for our pilots. We'll use our local networks. Fortunately, you speak French, from what I have been told. We have some papers for you. You'll have guides at every step of the way. In case of problems in Switzerland, we will provide you with the address of the Australian authorities in Geneva and Bern. Meanwhile, we can accommodate you in a building near here."

"Thank you so much. But I have a friend here."

"Be careful nonetheless."

I slowly walked down the corridor towards the exit, pensive and impressed by all the bustling activity. Each office was like a buzzing hive. Women and men in uniform, moving from room to room, maps on walls, transmission equipment, even a radio studio.

I was walking down the stairs when I came face to face with her.

"Louise, what are you doing here?"

"And you, my love?"

What joy! My heart leapt in my chest. It had been so long since I had held her in my arms. We exchanged a long, long kiss. We could not let go of each other. We stood there in the middle of the stairs. Nobody dared to intervene. They waited patiently for the end of our long embrace.

"Louise, was it you who made me come here?"

"No, but I knew you were on your way... to join me, no? I'll collect my things and we'll go to my place. Wait for me downstairs."

Was it not wonderful to be waited for like that? My dark thoughts vanished in an instant.

Louise lived in a small flat in Notting Hill, on the first floor. In the main room, a bow window opened onto a small garden at the back.

"Tell me, Louise, what were you doing at the SOE? I thought you were at the University of London?"

"I was at first, but then... well, as you had told me, our military is very interested in nuclear research. You always defend the idea that researchers must be in the service of their country, especially in times of war. So that's why I am at the SOE."

"Can you tell me what the SOE is, exactly?"

"What about you? How did you end up on Baker Street?"

"I came to see you."

"Stop fooling around. You have another plan in mind, as always."

"I have to go to Switzerland to meet a chemist colleague who could help me obtain a substance capable of fighting stress."

"Oh, yes, stress. The way we react after being attacked. At the moment, there is certainly no shortage of attacks."

"Do you think the SOE will be able to help me?"

"You've come to the right place. I'll tell you, since you don't seem to know, the SOE aims at assisting the French Resistance against the Nazis on French soil. They have small networks throughout France that work to sabotage anything that might help the Germans and the Vichy government to develop their industry. On Dorset Square there's a special section of the French Resistance incorporated in the SOE They will help you to get to Switzerland. But why do you want to go? It's dangerous. I don't want to lose you!"

"I know the risks: everyone's told me since I made my decision."

"You don't realise, but you have to be wary of everyone. There are informers everywhere. Be careful at all times, don't talk too much."

"So you won't tell me anything? Will I ever know what you're doing at the SOE?"

"You I can tell. You're part of the NRC and you know what our work is about. Nuclear physics is the focus of intense discussion. The English are afraid that if the Germans ever come here, they will be very interested in what we are doing. I am negotiating, and we'll succeed, I'm sure, in getting nuclear research transferred to Canada. Guess where? McGill!"

"No! And I've come all this way to see you! And now you tell me you're going to Montreal, the way you stayed glued to your job at Laval in Quebec all those years! I'm out of luck, again!"

"In research, we have to evolve, we have to move, you know that as well as I do."

"Do you know how I'm going to get to Switzerland?"

"They will definitely parachute you in with other members of the SOE."

"But I've never parachuted."

"Don't worry; someone will carry you on his back."

Again, I could not sleep all night.

~ *CHAPTER 41* ~

The big day arrived. Why had I decided to leave? To join Louise, true. But I was not sure what compelled me to keep on going. The drive to acquire knowledge, and keep learning? A visceral need to push the research ahead?

The aircraft was even less comfortable than the one I had taken from Montreal. We were all equipped like real soldiers, paratroopers. I was amazed by the progress that had been made over the years. Fred had kept us informed of the aeronautical research he led at the NRC, but still I was scared stiff. I did not even know where we were going. The pilot and co-pilot were navigating by sight, regularly glancing at a map. The aircraft appeared to be losing altitude. We would soon have to jump. No, not yet. First he doubled back, gaining altitude again, and went straight for at least ten minutes before executing another loop. I recognised the place we had passed earlier. In almost total darkness, torch beams appeared. The plane gained altitude again and suddenly the door opened. Wind entered the cabin. It was time to jump. I was attached to a man whose name I did not even know. I hoped that this was not his first jump. Then… emptiness. The fall lasted only a few seconds and the parachute opened majestically, without a sound. The landing was smooth.

One after the other the parachutes landed as in a ballet, with no false steps. No time to contemplate the landscape. We had to quickly collect our gear and hide.

Men with guns took charge of us. They spoke French. They pointed to a house on top of a hill. That was where we had to go. The excitement of arrival had passed. We were told that we were only a few kilometres from the border, in the French Jura, and all things being equal, the coast was clear. I was the only one who would cross the border, the next day. People were waiting for me there.

The parachute jump having gone well, I was calmer. Few words were exchanged. We congratulated each other and wished each other good luck. I left my companions, accompanied by two armed men who seemed to know the way. There was a pine forest to cross. And then there was another group awaiting my arrival.

"Welcome to Switzerland. You will put on these clothes, Mr. Mont d'Or, because now you are an Australian diplomat. We will take you to the station. You have a direct train to Zurich. Here is your ticket. If you have any trouble, you have the addresses in Geneva and Bern. Unfortunately, we have no correspondent in Zurich."

Here, there was no sense of wartime. Yet Switzerland was in the middle of war-torn Europe. The Federal Swiss Institute of Technology was nothing like our North American campuses, a cluster of buildings, typical of German-speaking Switzerland in the last century, or even earlier. This by no means prevented them from doing fine research. The chemical laboratory of Leopold Ruzicka was world famous. Vladimir asked me no questions about how I had managed to get to Zurich. In Zagreb he had adopted the practise of discretion, simply waiting for the other to reveal his secrets.

"Thanks for welcoming me, Vladimir. I remember the very interesting discussion we had in Montreal. You told me about a compound that facilitates molecules' penetration of tissues. That's why I'm here."

"We have indeed made significant progress on adamantane and managed to produce the molecule last year. If it's not a secret, you could give me the chemical composition of the substance Hans referred to in his letter. He wrote me recently to say you were on your way. I can synthesise the compound in less than a week."

I knew the molecule's structure by heart. Wasn't that what I had come all this distance for?

"Quite true that it isn't difficult to graft adamantane onto an amino acid. Why don't we start right away?" said Vladimir, his eyes sparkling with eagerness.

Two days later, Vladimir presented me with a small vial containing white powder.

"Here is your product, Paul. I am doing this for Hans and for the sake of research. You know that his parents once helped me. I owe them this much. I'm also giving you the production recipe. It isn't complicated and any organic chemist, or biochemist like you, can do the coupling, provided of course that you have a suitable laboratory. Which reminds me, Paul, we're having a small reception tonight in the laboratory. I hope that you are free and can join us."

"I have nothing special on tonight. I'd be delighted!"

In fact, I had no idea how long I was going to be staying in Zurich.

Vladimir introduced me to the head of the laboratory, the third Nobel Prize laureate I had the fortune to meet. Prof. Ruzicka was a scholar. He too came from Zagreb. He knew several languages, including Dutch, which he had learned during a training course in Utrecht. He also spoke excellent English, with only a hint of an accent.

"Vladimir told me that you have worked with Drs. Banting and McLeod. What a great discovery, insulin! And Professor Collip, an excellent biochemist. I hope he doesn't work on terpenes and steroid hormones like us. We are already struggling to maintain competition with the Kendall group at the Mayo Clinic in the United States. In this regard, I would like to introduce a colleague who works in Basel, Professor Tadeusz Reichstein. In these difficult times, you will understand that it is better to work in Switzerland than in any other European country."

When it came to talking about hormones, lengthy introductions were not necessary. Passion quickly took over.

"As you have done in Canada, we've used numerous extracts to isolate hormones," said Reichstein. "For us it is the adrenal. In this little gland we have already isolated many steroids, some of which are active."

"I followed your work, first on vitamin C, which I prescribed to some of my patients when I was practising in Melbourne, then naturally your discovery of deoxycorticosterone or cortisone, which protects the survival of animals after removal of the adrenals."

"I heard the Germans were giving pilots adrenal extracts to enhance their performance."

"Not to my knowledge, though it is possible, considering the effects of adrenal hormones. But if we succeeded with extracts of pancreas, I think it is preferable to administer purified hormones, as you are doing. In addition, we often observe resistance to treatment. This is why I work on anti-hormones in Montreal."

Vladimir had joined the conversation.

"Paul, could we ask you a favour? We have no choice but to publish in national journals such as *Helvetica Chimica Acta*. Right now, we cannot afford to send items outside the borders by mail. Since you have to return to London, might you take this article of Professor Reichstein's on vitamins and hormones? The publisher requested it before the war. Its publication is of utmost importance to us, and to all those who, like yourself, are interested in hormones."

"I'll do my best, but I do not know the exact date of my return."

I was unable to give them any information in this regard, especially as I did not myself know how or when I would be able to return to London. But how exciting it was to see that researchers could remain so enthusiastic, despite the difficulties caused by the war!

~ *CHAPTER 42* ~

I had two contact addresses, in Bern and in Geneva. The Bern address was the Australian Embassy. I would stagnate if I stayed there for the whole war. Geneva was the unknown. I chose the unknown. Twice, on the train from Zurich to Geneva, I was asked for my papers, but despite my apprehensions, everything went well. In Geneva, I took a tram to the indicated address. A name on the door: Philippe Monod. I rang. No answer. I decided to come back later. In the meantime, I went for a walk on the shores of Lake Geneva, calm, majestic and surrounded by the snowy peaks of the French Alps. I inhaled deeply. Clean air at last! I sat at a bar by the lake. I closed my eyes for a moment. I felt a presence beside me.

"Hello. May I sit at your table?"

"I do not believe I have the honour of knowing you."

"But I know you, Monsieur Mont d'Or."

It took me a moment to collect my thoughts. I had forgotten that this was my new name.

"You know my name?"

"I was waiting for you. Philippe Monod."

"You scared me."

"I saw you ring my doorbell. For security reasons, I did not answer, and followed you instead. It is easier to talk here. You know, there are spies everywhere, even in Geneva. It is a hub between so-called free Switzerland and occupied France. Before I leave, I will set a piece of paper on the table here with the address of a place where you can sleep tonight and a meeting spot for tomorrow when you go back across the border. I also have information for you to give to my brother Jacques, Jacques Monod. He lives in an old building at 26, rue Monsieur le Prince in Paris, fourth floor, no lift. You'll serve as a liaison, if you don't object. You know rue Monsieur le Prince, I imagine?"

"Not at all. I've never been to Paris, unfortunately. But I have been to France before. I was in the trenches of the Somme and then I was transferred to Marseilles before sailing back to Australia. Last week was my second time in France, but that was only a dark road and a forest."

"Well you still have many things to see. You may be disappointed in Paris as it is now. Rue Monsieur le Prince is near the Luxembourg Gardens, behind the medical school. Not far from the Sorbonne. Be careful. Do not go see my brother directly after you arrive. Tomorrow, when you leave, you will be given an address in Paris and new papers. Foreign diplomats, especially British diplomats, are not well regarded in France at the moment."

In the late afternoon, I went to the agreed upon meeting place, a bus stop several kilometres from Geneva. I waited. Suddenly a police car stopped in front of me. A policeman got out. I felt my heart begin to gallop.

"Are you waiting for the bus? Don't you know that the last one passed over an hour ago? Where do you have to go? Can we take you somewhere?"

"No thank you, I am not waiting for the bus. I... I have a date with my girlfriend."

It was the first sentence that came to mind.

"In that case... we'll leave you."

Fortunately, they did not ask for my papers. Stress... that feeling of discomfort that seizes your entrails, then tachycardia, cold sweat... I did not have time to think any longer, for another vehicle slowed down and stopped in front of me.

"Mont d'Or, get in the back and duck down."

The vehicle took off quickly. I spent a good half-hour with my head down, not knowing where we were going, though I sensed the car was climbing upwards. It stopped. I got out and realised that I was not alone.

"We'll cross the border now. On the other side, the FTP will be waiting. We will give you other clothes, less identifiable. The FTP comrades will help you get to the places you need to go. Good luck, comrades... and long live freedom..."

So there I was, in France again. We met a group of women and children, each wearing a yellow star. No noise, not a glance exchanged. A stone house. Soup waiting for us.

"Mont d'Or? You will be supported by the Stockbroker network. The rest will follow. Take care of yourself. Don't talk to anyone. Good luck."

Looking at my new papers, I discovered that I was born in St. Claude in the Jura. I was a teacher. We travelled in a covered truck and took the country roads. However, not far from Dole, the driver suddenly veered onto a path to the right.

"Shit, a Kraut convoy. Hide!"

I had never heard the word but I understood immediately that it meant the Germans. Five trucks preceded by motorcycles. They had not seen us. We could continue. Enemy checkpoints and convoys forced us to make detours to Dijon. I was put on a train to Paris and told that I should only show my papers if asked, and not to speak.

In the compartment with me was a family with two young children. There were three passport checks in a row. We always heard the same words, starting at the front of the car. "*Ausweis papiere bitte.*" Each time, the German looked at me, observing me: a few seconds of intense anxiety and then relief when the compartment door closed.

Arriving at the railway station was a nightmare. Could this be the Paris of my dreams, my father's Paris, a city of culture if ever there was one? There were signs in German everywhere, in Gothic script. Awful. I wanted to vomit. I was weeping inside. Around the station was no better. German soldiers everywhere, with forbidding faces. Montreal was very far away.

For the next three days, I did not leave the flat that I had been lent in the twentieth district, near the rue de Menilmontant. Yet in this working-class neighbourhood, the atmosphere was more breathable than around the station. Queues at food stores and children shouting as they rattled down the street on their skates with metal wheels. I was told to take bus number 96 to get to the Latin Quarter. There were few people on the rear platform, yet it wasn't cold. I bought a ticket that the controller passed through a machine attached to his belt and then pulled on the bell, indicating to the driver that he could start driving again. Paris, here you are at last! For so long I have been seeing you in my dreams. Since childhood, I have wished I could see you, with tricolour flags on the windows, elegant women with parasols and genteel men walking arm-in-arm down the boulevards. Unfortunately it was not like that at all. People would not look at each other or talk. No attempt at conversation on the bus. A swastika flag flew over City Hall – how awful! Finally the Seine, Notre Dame, the Left Bank, the Latin Quarter. I got off the bus at Odeon, near rue Monsieur le Prince. I heard gunshots. Two young men with red armbands were being chased by men in trench coats holding their hats so they would not fly away.

"Boche bastards," said an old man watching the scene.

Rue Monsieur le Prince was a little street sloping upwards. Number 26 was just as it had been described to me. I walked up the stairs and met a young man running down. He must have been used to it. Four flights of stairs! I was out of breath. We did not have this type of house in Canada, Australia or anywhere else I knew of. Narrow, two doors. No names. Right or left? Right. I knocked quietly. No answer. Left, then. Still nothing. Jacques was probably at work. His brother had not even told me what he did for a living. I was about to head back downstairs when I heard a door open.

"Paul?"

"Yes."

"Come in quickly so I can close the door."

~ *CHAPTER 43* ~

The flat was quite spacious. This was unusual for such a young occupant, perhaps fifteen years younger than me. Musical scores were scattered everywhere. A cello leaned up against the wall.

"You called me Paul just now. I thought that in France, young people are more formal with their elders."

"But you're young, Paul, flamboyant and full of life! Do you like music?"

"Yes, as much as anyone, but unfortunately, I never learned to play an instrument. I'm interested in many things but my job doesn't leave time for music. And to be a good musician takes time."

"That's true, but everything is possible. Just organise things the way you want and take life as it comes. I learned the arts from my father, who is a painter. My mother is English. Or I should say, Scottish. Here I am, rambling on... Did you see my brother?"

"Yes, a charming man. He looks quite well. We did not have much of an exchange. Unfortunately, we did not spend much time together."

"Even if he lives in Geneva, where our family stayed during

the first war, and he knows many people, he is very mistrustful."

"That is not unwise, from what he told me. He gave me this letter for you."

"I will open it later. I know a lot of things about you, Paul."

"I thought I was here as a secret agent."

"There are no secrets for researchers."

"What do you mean researchers? Don't tell me you work in a laboratory too!"

"Oh, yes! I hesitated between being a concert musician and a biologist. I chose biology."

"A fatal error, perhaps! And what do you do?"

"I work near here, at the Sorbonne. I am a biochemist. I work on metabolism, enzymes. And you, I know, are trying to characterise biological molecules. Two different schools of biochemistry."

"You, the French are *tannants*, as they say in Quebec. Tiresome, as we say! All wrapped up in your semantic quarrels. Look at what's happening on the other side of the Atlantic."

"We are waiting for the Americans to come to visit us. The Canadians too, as in the previous war," Jacques replied dryly.

"Yes thank you, I was here, in the trenches of the Somme. I almost lost a leg."

"Me too, imagine. I almost lost a leg to polio. But we are wandering off topic. I am familiar with American research. Pragmatic. Concrete and well-funded, which isn't the case here."

"In the committee I sit on in Canada, we have the same problem and our President, James Collip, wishes to grant scholarships to students. He wants research to be recognised as a real profession, and for our universities to be more effective."

"When this war is over, I hope with an Allied victory, that it is the type of policy we must uphold all over the world. The James Collip you mention, is he the same one who isolated insulin and works on hormones?"

"I see that you are well-informed."

"I read, and I spent some time at Caltech, California, in Morgan's laboratory, which is not only interested in genetics but also hormones."

"Really? So you worked in a lab in the United States?"

"I almost became an orchestra conductor in Pasadena. Biologist or musician, it's all the same fight."

His humour and compelling eloquence raised my spirits.

"Tell me, Jacques, what makes genetics and the enzymes you work on so exciting?"

"Good question. Isn't it fascinating to study the real mechanisms of life? Look, in order to function, an enzyme must absolutely recognise its partner; remember it like a loved one. Listen carefully: E. Coli, which is particularly studied by André Lwoff here at the Pasteur Institute, can metabolise the sugar necessary to its growth through enzymatic activity. I have observed that one lump of sugar can block the action of another and thus decrease its effect. Lwoff calls this, enzyme adaptation."

"In Montreal, with Hans Selye, we invented a name for the general adaptation syndrome that we are studying: stress."

"What?"

And then nothing could stop me. We talked for hours, in another world, on another planet. We forgot what was happening around us. Then it was four in the morning.

"I have to go home, Jacques."

"Certainly not. It is forbidden to be on the streets of Paris at night. You'll stay here and tomorrow there will be light."

It had been daytime for a long time when we opened our eyes again.

"Damn," said Jacques, "I forgot that I had to seed my bacteria. Do you want to come to the lab with me?"

"With pleasure!"

The Sorbonne, that magical place my father had so often talked about, the workplace of Claude Bernard and many of his students! The laboratory, quite dilapidated, was on the second floor, staircase E.

"How do you continue to work while the city is infested with Germans?"

"Therein lies the art and the quality of the French."

I was fascinated by this man who whistled tunes from works by Bach and Schubert while handling bacteria.

Suddenly we heard a noise. A student was running up the stairs four at a time. He said, gasping for breath, "Hide! The Gestapo's downstairs. I heard they're looking for you, Jacques."

"Paul, put on this white coat and come with me into the bacteria room."

The laboratory door opened with a crash. Shouts and loud voices were heard.

"Does Jacques Monod work here?"

"Yes," said one of the assistants.

"We want to see him. Go get him, and don't tell me he isn't here. Understand?"

"Gentlemen, what is the meaning of this? What do you want from me?" Jacques asked from the end of the corridor.

"You must come with us."

"I'm sorry; I'm in mid experiment. If I come with you now, you will all be contaminated. You know we work with extremely dangerous microbes! What I have in this box could kill you! You saw what is written on the door: 'radioactivity'. So if you stay here much longer without a lab coat and other protection, I can only foresee certain death."

Clearly Jacques's bluff had its effect. The three Gestapo officers left without further ado, slamming the door behind them, and swearing: *Satan, der Teufel*... the devil.

~ *CHAPTER 44* ~

I wasn't sure I could bear the situation any longer. Living in a city where you cannot look at the person in front of you without imagining that he wishes you harm was unthinkable. Beautiful as the city was, the walls had ears and, on every street corner and in every home, someone could denounce you. We left the Sorbonne separately. Jacques told me not to go straight home to avoid being followed. We agreed to meet at my flat two days later. He thought it was safer there.

I wanted to see the Eiffel Tower. I thought it unwise to take public transport. It seemed safer to walk. That way, I had a better chance of escaping if the militia stopped me. I had no documents on me, only my papers in the name of Paul Mont d'Or, a teacher from St. Claude… and a tourist in Paris, I added mentally.

Unfortunately, access to the tower was prohibited. I had to content myself with contemplating it from afar. There were no patrols, no identity checks all day.

As we had agreed, Jacques came to see me two days later.

"So what did you do yesterday?"

"I visited Paris, the Eiffel Tower, and the Arc de Triomphe."

"You're crazy! You passed right by the Gestapo headquarters!"

"It seems easier to live in Paris while walking rather than hiding."

"That may be… So I have good news and bad news, which would you like first?"

"Bad news first. That's what people always say, isn't it?"

"Well, you cannot go to London."

"What do you mean? I absolutely must go back! I have an extremely important document to give to someone there."

"Yes, I know. Everything about our present activities is important. But the problem is that we don't know how to get agents from France to England. Do you understand?"

"So what is the good news?"

"You're on the wanted list, as a British counter-espionage agent."

"You must be joking!"

"Not at all. The German authorities believe that you went to Switzerland to collect information on biological warfare. In addition, you are engaged to a nuclear specialist, and our German friends would love to learn more about the use of nuclear weapons. They drove all their scholars out, and now there's nobody left in their country that can help in this regard."

"But I'm not engaged, or even married."

"Well, for them it's as if you were."

"I hope that Louise isn't in danger?"

"Now that's a question I cannot answer."

"So what do I do?"

"Here is the real good news. Maybe you are not aware, but France is divided in two. Here in Paris, we are very lucky, we are under the double protection of the Nazis and Vichy, while further south, France is still free, though probably not for much longer. Just go. I think you have understood that I can help you. I know a lot of people. So you will take the train from the Bastille station. It's a local train that will take you to Brie Comte Robert. There, a car will be waiting for you. It will take you to the demarcation line, and you can go south. Don't worry about me, I'll be fine. If one day our scientific paths cross again, we will talk more about the battles we must wage to better understand the mysteries of life. In the meantime, you must be very careful."

"Listen, Jacques, I have a favour to ask. I have a manuscript that a Swiss chemist gave me. He wants it published in London. Anyway, that won't happen overnight. It may take some time."

"Give it to me anyway. It is easier to get documents through borders than men."

I left Paris with a heavy heart. Although it was not the Paris of my dreams, I had finally reached the goal I had set myself so many years ago: to see the capital of France.

I had to cross the River Loire. I had understood from the beginning that the French Resistance network had taken charge of me. And also used me, perhaps. But I had got what I wanted, and so had they. I did not quite understand what the FTP, the FFI or the MUR were, or even the role of the SOE in the whole affair. To think that I could have stayed at McGill, quietly doing my experiments with Hans, publishing results, and participating in discussions at the NRC in Ottawa! What I was doing now was from vanity, to show that I could get what I wanted from the Swiss researchers. Or perhaps to prove something to Louise? She who was so brilliant, and who one day would be head of nuclear research in her country.

There I was, facing the Loire. How can it be harder to cross a few hundred metres of river between Saint-Denis-de-l'Hôtel and Jargeau than cross the St. Lawrence, in Quebec, borne by blocks of ice like the ones they carve at Carnival? But it was difficult to reach the south bank of the Loire without getting shot. However, the Resistance fighters had many schemes. I became Monsieur Teacher, taking a group of school children across the river to Mass in the only church that had not been destroyed by recent bombings. In front of heavily armed French militiamen and German soldiers, I quietly crossed the Loire with my 'pupils' without anyone asking me a thing.

South of Jargeau, we entered Sologne and had a well-deserved night's rest. The journey continued without incident. Each time, I was accompanied by one or more men from different networks. Was I such an important person? Then it was the train again. Going south, towards the sun. No, how could it be? Back to Marseilles!

~ *CHAPTER 45* ~

Jacques had planned everything, organised everything. Upon my arrival at St. Charles Station, I was brought to the university, nearby. Colonnaded buildings, like the ancient Greek temples. On the frieze above the triglyphs, an inscription in gold letters: *Biology Laboratory, Chemistry and Physics.*

"Here you will be undisturbed," said the university President in welcoming me. "We've put a small laboratory at your disposal. I was told you are a biochemist. If you could train one or two students while you're here, it would be a great boon for our university."

Caught off guard, I could not refuse. But what was I to do? The laboratory was decently appointed, but more oriented to chemistry than biology. The students were about to arrive and I had no idea of what I was going to say.

"Gentlemen, since you will be with me for some time and I'm supposed to teach you something, I wonder if you would be interested in chemical synthesis?"

As there was no response, I assumed that they agreed. So I asked them to find me the necessary equipment. I wanted to replicate what Vladimir and I had done in Zürich: coupling adamantane with my compound. I had the ingredients; they only needed to be prepared.

A few weeks later I had obtained a significant amount of anti-hormone. To be soluble, it had to be diluted in dimethyl sulfoxide. But, as is often the case in research, I began to have doubts. What if all I had done to acquire this product was useless, if the product was ineffective or still toxic? I had to be absolutely sure. Then I thought, why should I not get my students to help?

"Tell me, what if we did a bit of physiology for a change? Do you know if one can obtain laboratory animals here? Rats in particular?"

"Rats? There are plenty in the docks."

A burst of laughter.

"Very funny, but don't you have a better idea?"

"Maybe we could go ask in Biology. We have friends there."

"Go and see them. Tell them that we would need about twenty rats."

I did not see my students for the rest of the day.

"Where have you been? I've been waiting for hours!"

"Excuse me, Professor, but the rats... we don't want to touch them."

"Come on! They won't eat you! Have you at least found some?"

"Uh, yes, in the physiology department. And the instructors will let you have them, provided they can do the experiments with you. They've heard about your work in Canada."

"Well, have them come and we will do it all together!"

The three physiologists knew about our work on insulin and new pituitary hormones. But they had not had any previous opportunity to study these facets because of the war and financial duress.

In a short time, we managed to build a laboratory for studying the stress response in animals.

Isolated in its cage, the rat explored, frightened by the slightest noise and behaving as if it had just arrived in an unfamiliar place, anxious and distressed. We noted with amazement that rats did not exhibit this behaviour after receiving an anti-hormone injection.

So I won my bet. The anti-hormone could block stress: it was an anti-stress substance, just as we had imagined in Montreal! We repeated the experiments by putting the animals in different conditions in the new environment. Each time the result was the same. That was all one could say for the moment.

One day, it was a Tuesday morning, there were noises in the hall like the ones I had heard outside Jacques Monod's laboratory at the Sorbonne.

"Those who have something to fear, hide quickly!" said one of my physiologist colleagues. "I'm going to see what's happening. Put everything on a bench."

I could not afford to expose myself, given my irregular status at the university. But, hidden behind a door, it was easy for me to hear the voices in the corridor.

"We need to see Professor Mont d'Or."

"He isn't here today."

"Can you give him this envelope? Thank you."

They left as they had come.

My colleague gave me the letter. I opened it.

'*Come to 3 rue Molière this evening. The street is near the old port and runs alongside the Opera. Old building, third floor, right door. We'll explain. Destroy this letter as soon as you've read it. SOE Network Gardener.*'

"Were they Germans?" I asked.

"No, but they weren't French either. They had English accents. The Gestapo or militia are easy to recognise. These ones weren't Gestapo, for sure."

We had no more time to do experiments that day. Everyone understood that very well.

The Opera's Greek temple architecture loomed behind high iron gates. My forehead was beaded with sweat. Number 3, rue Molière. Sinister. A staircase with potholed steps. Third floor, no lift, so you could not walk up without being noticed. The right door opened. Suddenly someone pulled me inside and assured me I had not been followed. The only light came from a hanging bulb with no shade. I had trouble seeing the faces of the three men facing me.

One of them approached me and said in English,

"Paul, don't be afraid. We're with the Marseilles SOE and are in touch with the French Resistance networks. We've learned the Gestapo is looking for you. Someone denounced you, but no one knows who. One of our agents was told it was because you wouldn't reveal the formula for a chemical substance whose purpose we didn't quite understand. You must leave Marseilles. We'll tell you when. Until then, be very careful."

I felt constantly spied on, even in the laboratory. Yet everything worked. The experiments moved ahead, with excellent results. Twice a week, I went to the Timone hospital with a bag of rat corpses to be incinerated. All my senses alert, I avoided the Canebière. I took small, narrow streets to avoid being spotted. One day I felt I was being followed. Suddenly, something hard was planted in the middle of my back.

"Up against the wall and don't look behind you. Don't move."

"What do you want?"

"Your money. Where is it?"

"Here, in the bag."

The whole episode had not lasted more than a minute. I saw the two thugs rush into an alley with my bag of dead rats. I laughed, thinking of their faces when they opened their bag of loot.

Soon after, I found a note on my desk: 'Tonight, in the laboratory'. All my colleagues were gone. I remained on the premises, claiming I had an article to write. I waited. There was a knock. I opened the door.

"Good evening, Paul. We're taking you into the scrub, the *maquis* as we call it, near Antibes, where another network will take charge of you. You'll board a felucca with a Polish crew. Out at sea, a submarine is waiting."

"To take me back to England?"

"No, to Corsica."

"Corsica? That's crazy, what am I going to do in Corsica?"

"You'll stay there, waiting for better days. Let's go. Do you have your things?"

"But what about my experiments?"

"They'll wait, like everything else."

~ *CHAPTER 46* ~

Again, everything had been well organised. Through the *maquis*, we made our way down to the sea. Before a stony cove, well concealed, a felucca and three sailors awaited us. I boarded the boat, wishing my companions good luck.

The trip lasted only a few minutes. The moon's white light was reflected on a calm, still sea. Suddenly a monster rose before my eyes, a huge black mass that shattered the water's surface. A powerful wave all but capsized the felucca. Then the monster was perfectly still and silent before me, as if watching me. A trap door opened in the middle of its back. I imagined a swarm of little monsters scrambling out to ambush me. But instead it was our felucca that approached the monster and pulled alongside an iron ladder.

"Welcome aboard the *Casabianca*, a French Navy submarine. You're the last one we had to collect. We can leave now."

I had used many means of transport in my life, but never had I imagined that I would ride in a submarine one day. I felt very uneasy, trapped underwater. What if an enemy submarine spotted us? To die in such conditions... I tried not to think about it. I was hot. My heart was pounding in my ears, my throat was parched and I had a knot in my stomach, all symptoms of stress.

I could not eat. I lay prostrate on a makeshift bed. I did not want to talk. I must have dozed off. I was a prisoner, bound hand and foot, and about to be thrown overboard... but no. A low knock on the door wrenched me out of my bad dream.

"We're almost there," said a sailor.

"Thank you. What time is it?"

"About five o'clock."

"Where are we?"

"In the Gulf of Ajaccio. We're waiting for a signal from the beach. Captain Herminier raised the periscope. It may take some time, for reasons of safety."

The sun was beginning to rise behind the mountains. The door opened onto a breathtaking landscape and the scent of rock roses, thyme and herbs of the *maquis*. This was the perfume of Corsica, people said, the same I had briefly inhaled on my voyage back to Australia on the *Osmonde* at the end of the last war. I remembered it as if it had been yesterday. The years had passed, and again it was wartime.

Two feluccas came to meet us. I boarded one while three men, fully engaged in their trans-shipment, unloaded an impressive number of weapons.

"Attentu a ùnfà le cascà. Pèsanu." [4]

One of them addressed me in Corsican.

"Verghja, più bella marina di u mondu. Benvinutu in Corsica,"[5] he said, pointing to a white sandy beach, divided in two by a majestic pine forest.

---

[4] Be careful not to drop them. They're heavy.

[5] Verghia, the most beautiful beach in the world. Welcome to Corsica.

Other armed men were waiting on the beach. In less than five minutes, every trace of our passage was eliminated. Everything had been loaded in record time into two sheeted vehicles.

"*Collaprestu qui.*"[6]

A few minutes later, shaken by the jolts of the truck that rattled down the road, winding steeply up, and lined with giant eucalyptus, we arrived in front of a cluster of stone buildings. Some were in ruins but nonetheless forbidding.

"Welcome to the penitentiary of Coti-Chiavari," the young man said in French. He was armed to the teeth.

"The what? Am I a prisoner?"

"No, don't worry. It's a prison but it hasn't been used for nearly half a century. We don't use it to lock up convicts but just to keep a few weapons, the ones we are given for the Corsican Resistance. We are quite well organised, you'll see. And even on the continent, when people hide in the mountains they still say they've 'taken to the bush'. We'll take you to a safe place, the grandfather's *oriu*. You will stay there for a while."

"What is the grandfather's *oriu*?"

"A kind of cave carved in granite in the middle of the *maquis*. You'll be with other fugitive Resistance workers. The grandfather of one of them used to sleep down there so he could get up at dawn to go hunting."

"*Porta di oriu read the sin'ababbonu!*"[7]

It was not exactly a luxury hotel. Mattresses lay on the bare stone floor. A large fireplace opened towards the outside for cooking. There was no electricity. The 'toilets' were a hundred metres below. The only great advantage was a magnificent

---

[6]Climb quickly.

[7] Take him to the grandfather's grotto!

view over the Gulf of Ajaccio, the tip of Isolella peninsula and, at the very bottom, the city of Ajaccio.

And again that sweet fragrance. I remember a passage from Maupassant,'*La Corse, enveloppée dans une sorte de voile léger. Et le soleil se leva, dessinant toutes les saillies en ombres noires*'[8]

My companions were much younger than me. They had the fire of youth, the rage to fight the enemy. Do battle, sabotage, and kill the invaders, the Italian Blackshirts.

For weeks I watched their preparations for large-scale actions in the Ajaccio region. It was only May but already hot. The *oriu* was an ideal place for avoiding the heat. And we were quite well fed. We never knew the menu ahead of time. It was frugal, almonds, semolina cakes from broad bean flour, chestnut flour cakes. On lucky days, we had wild boar, pig or goat that we had to carve ourselves. You never asked where they came from. There was also *brocciu*, fresh cheese made from the whey of sheep's milk. I had some when I arrived. But it grew rare and then disappeared completely. I later learned that this was not due to any fault of the shepherd's, or his sudden disappearance, but simply to the fact that the ewes did not give milk in summer.

I had pretty well adapted to the living conditions, but inaction was beginning to weigh on me. Except for treating some minor injuries, I felt useless.

---

[8]Corsica, covered with a light veil of mist. The sun rose behind it, outlining the jagged crests like black shadows.

~ *CHAPTER 47* ~

One day some armed men arrived, led by another who was clearly someone important. "Hello, my name is Jean Nicoli and I am the leader of the National Front, the main Resistance organisation in Corsica. Allow me to introduce Charlot and Ribello. The comrades told me about you, they said you were working for British counter-espionage."

"That's a pretty fancy expression, but since that's what everyone thinks..."

"Our SOE comrades in Marseilles have told us you are a scientist and also bilingual. A scientist is also an engineer. Can you make explosives?"

"No, unfortunately, they are not my specialty. There are scientists and there are scientists. I am only interested in the human body. If you need a doctor, I can help you."

"If necessary, we will certainly ask for your help. Meanwhile, you will serve as liaison between the Resistance fighters and the British networks preparing to land in Corsica to drive back the Italians."

Before going on their way, our visitors and some of the men who were with us sang *A Sampiera*, the song of the National Front, in chorus:

"Siatte Cors'e Francesi, tutt'all'arme Corsi 'arditi, morti, li morti has numighi."[9]

This is how I became an intelligence officer for the next few months. I learned by radio the codes I needed to transmit information to Allied troops still in Morocco and Algeria. The messages I had to send made me laugh. 'Sardine is exclusively homo', meaning 'men can be parachuted' or 'Homo to perform on goat', the code for 'Land ready, light signals OK'.

Resistance fighters prepared for the protection of roads and strategic locations, as well as airdrops of weapons. Alas, this work was not without risks: many never returned from their mission. German repression was becoming increasingly tough. Our *oriu* was a refuge, away from the road and well protected by weapons and the dense scrubland. But some of our residents disappeared forever.

I decided to set up a makeshift clinic and treat the injured as best I could. Some women 'from the family' as they were called, also came to talk to me about their problems. One night I was called to the village of Coti-Chiavari for a birth, a little 'Dume'.

One day, with great consternation, we learned that Jean Nicoli had been arrested in his house in Ajaccio. But nothing could stop the Corsican Resistance, wounded, tortured in its flesh. Bombings and sabotage ensued. Jean was executed. He would never see the day of his country's liberation. Indeed, events accelerated during that summer of '43. First came the attack on Sicily by North African Allied troops, then the capitulation of Mussolini and therefore of Italy, giving the

---

[9]Be Corsican and French! Take up your weapons, bold Corsicans! Death to the enemy.

signal for insurrection. The weather was hot and the drought extreme, with water shortages everywhere. But despite the difficulties, in several days the Resistance took back the island's strategic towns. Ajaccio was liberated on September 8, following a popular uprising, and then it was the turn of Sartene, Porto-Vecchio and finally Bastia on October 4. I needed to transmit a message: a battalion of more than a hundred men, sent from Algiers by General Giraud, was to arrive in Ajaccio on the *Casabianca*. Moroccan troops were expected, but also English and American ones. On the peninsula side, the Allies were heading north in Italy.

I was better informed of the troops' movements than I had been in the first war. I performed my duties as well as possible, and my transmission work with British and American troops in North Africa came to the attention of people in high places. One day, General de Gaulle arrived in Corsica, greeted by a cheering crowd. Corsica was the first French department to be liberated. We were at a turning point in the war.

"Paul, pack your things. You're leaving us. General de Gaulle agreed to take you back to London."

"I can't believe it!"

"It is true! *A qui sàaspetta, tuttughjunghje*. Everything comes to those who wait."

We embraced each other. Goodbye Corsica. I sang the end of the National Front song that I now knew by heart: *"Siatte Cors'e Francesi, tutt'all'arme Corsi 'arditi, morti, li morti has numighi."* I did not know then that they were all Communists.

"Ti ringrazziemu per ciochetehaifattu per noi e per a Corsica." [10]

---

[10]We thank you for what you have done for us and for Corsica.

~ *CHAPTER 48* ~

Destination: London, in the General's plane. This was particularly unexpected because De Gaulle's relations with the British were somewhat stormy. I was going to see Louise at last. Immediately, with no further ado! Straight to Baker Street and the SOE. It was close to General De Gaulle's area; his car left me there.

"Do you know where I can find Louise Leblanc?"

"Louise Leblanc? I don't know," said the young male attendant at reception.

"Do you think I'm an idiot?" I replied, annoyed. "She works here at the SOE."

"I've only been here for a few weeks. Give me your papers and sit down. I'll see what I can find out."

The minutes of waiting were interminable. The young man came back.

"I'm sorry, but I am told there is no one by that name here."

I was furious, holding myself from seizing him by the collar when two men appeared on their way out of the building. One of them I recognised.

"William Stephenson! Do you remember me? Paul Dormont. Mont d'Or. I am with the NRC in Canada."

"Paul Dormont? But I thought you were in Corsica?"

"Oh, you knew?"

"Yes, everyone knows everything here in Baker Street. Sherlock Holmes is just down the street, as you know."

"Then can tell you me where Louise Leblanc is?"

"Are you interested in her?"

"I see that the SOE doesn't know everything. Louise is my companion. So where is she? This gentleman tells me he doesn't know."

"It's true; she's not here... not any more."

"I hope nothing has happened to her?"

"You are very pale. Don't worry. She's returned to Canada, safe and sound. She had completed her mission in London."

I remembered my discussion with Jacques Monod in Paris, the pursuit of scientists, especially those who worked in nuclear weapons.

It was a blow to my heart. I had been so looking forward to seeing her, surprising her, as I had done so often. There remained only one thing for me to do: return to Canada. I now wanted to leave as quickly as possible, leave this Europe where not long ago I had so greatly yearned to be.

I hardly heard what William Stephenson was saying.

"By the way, thank you for all you have done. Don't worry. We'll help you leave, soon."

Indeed, the SOE did things well, as always. Two days later I was on a plane to Quebec, with short stopovers in Iceland and Halifax. The German air force was now on the Eastern Front, having deserted the Atlantic.

Back in Montreal, at last, for some peace and quiet after the 'stressful' events in Europe. I called Louise. No answer. I called her laboratory, again nothing. I rushed to Bert's in Westmount. Ray was there. She welcomed me with open arms, clearly relieved to see me back, safe and sound. I was helpless, exhausted, and unable to react. She asked me no questions. Bert was in Ottawa. Ray called him, told him the good news of my return.

"Ray, can I talk to him please?"

"Bert. Yes, I'm fine, but exhausted. I can't bear it; I can hardly talk to you. Do you know where Louise is?"

"Yes, she left for the United States, Nevada. I'll tell you when I return to Montreal in two days."

I slept for more than twenty-four hours. I had been without news of anyone for months. I had to find Hans. I hurried to McGill; he was there with his bike. Relieved, he threw his arms around me, in tears of joy.

"We were worried, you know. Where were you?"

"It's a little complicated in Europe at the moment. And when you are stuck for months in an underground cave house or a submarine, it is difficult to send postcards."

"What are you saying? There's no sea in Switzerland and even fewer cave houses. Are you sure you're well? Do you want me to take you to the doctor?"

"You think I'm insane, don't you? Come to the café and I'll tell you."

And I did; every last detail. The SOE, parachuting into France, crossing the border, Paris, the demarcation line, Marseilles, the *Casabianca* and Corsica. The Resistance, Jacques Monod. I forgot to tell him about Switzerland. It was Hans who brought it up.

"You see? I've forgotten even why I went to Europe. Yes, I have it, the anti-hormone that lowers the stress response."

"No, really?"

"I swear. Vladimir synthesised it for me in Zurich. A breeze."

"Is your molecule active?"

"I tested it when I was in Marseilles and the rats responded as expected."

"What, you carried out experiments in Marseilles? In wartime?"

"Well, you work in Montreal in wartime!"

"Paul, that's amazing! We have to get down to work. When?"

"As soon as I have found Louise."

"I heard she was working in the United States."

"So it's true what Bert said?"

"Yes, as a nuclear physicist. She is on a project called 'Manhattan'. You can imagine how many men would like to join her team, not only Mr. Paul Dormont."

Hearing my own name startled me. It was so long since anyone had used it, except for the last time in London.

"Stop quibbling. Tell me how I can contact her as fast as possible."

"How much will you give me?"

"I'm not joking, Hans. I can't take any more. I need to see her."

"It's true that you don't look well. You know, after the alarm stage of stress, there's adaptation, and then exhaustion... before the recovery stage. Don't worry about Louise. The NRC sent her there, as they had sent her to London. She returns to Montreal this weekend and goes to Ottawa on Monday to give us a progress report. Naturally, you are invited because in case you have forgotten, you are still on the committee. And you too will give the NRC the results of your research."

Louise returned to Montreal as planned. We spent the whole weekend huddled tightly together, overjoyed to be together again, at last. We did not even think to open the curtains, indifferent to the blazing colours of the maple trees on Mount Royal. The war seemed far away, and yet...

I now knew more about Hans's scientific activities than about those of Bert, who was working somewhat less on his experiments. He had decided to make Canada a great country of science, with research centres and universities of equal calibre to those in the United States and some countries of Europe. Canada had been spared by the war, which gave it an edge over its European rivals.

My months in Europe had led me to ask myself what I would work on next. I could not make a decision immediately. I asked the McGill chemistry lab to manufacture the molecule prepared in Zurich. Obtaining adamantane was difficult but its coupling with the basic chemical structure posed no problem. Nor did solubilisation. The first tests in Hans's laboratory confirmed the results I had obtained in Marseilles. But, alas, we still did not know what organ it acted upon.

The trips to Ottawa gave me a feeling of freedom. I could take the train without the constant stress of being asked for papers, fear of arrest or denunciation on account of the slightest false move. During my hectic, back-and-forth trips in war-torn Europe, I had always been afraid of not using the right word in French, or giving myself away with an English or Québécois intonation. For a long time after, I had the same feeling of unease each time I got on a train.

According to the news that reached us from Europe, trains were leaving for Germany and Poland crowded with hundreds, perhaps thousands of people, Jews and Resistance fighters, or both, on a trip of no return. In Ottawa, we closely followed the development of the war in Europe and the Pacific. The country was so huge. Australia too was fighting, against the Japanese.

During our meetings, reports from military authorities took up much of our discussion time. Bert tried, often in vain, to talk about the future. But for many of us, the only thing that mattered was the present.

And for me, what mattered was Louise.

~ *CHAPTER 49* ~

On August 6, 1945 an atomic bomb fell on Hiroshima, and three days later, another bomb fell on Nagasaki Harbour in Kyushu, Japan. They devastated the country and ravaged the population, leaving thousands of people dead or wounded. Japan capitulated. Now I understand why Louise had gone to the United States so often. There was a closely guarded military secret that she had not told me. So much was unspoken during that war. And I started to think that it must have been the same during the first war too. Monash had certainly not told me everything. Those secrets I would never know.

"Louise, why didn't you tell me that you were making an atomic bomb?"

"I did not make a bomb. I would never have agreed to that. The Americans did as the NRC in Canada. They gathered a group of experts in nuclear physics to discuss the possibilities of nuclear fusion. It was not just the Americans, either. There were scholars from the Allied countries, British, French and even Australian. And great scientists, mostly Jews expelled from Europe. I think very few of us would have imagined that our skills would lead to this horror."

"It's hard to say, but maybe otherwise we would still be at war with the Japanese."

"That's what I am trying to convince myself of."

"Personally, I have not participated in sabotage or killed anyone. And yet I have indirectly helped the Corsican Resistance to fight the Italian and German troops, and there were injuries and deaths. War is dirty. Nothing can be done. Try to remember, think of the future, our future."

"What do you mean?"

"Since our atoms hooked together, and my positive ions are attracted to your negative ions, don't you think we could merge?"

"You mean combine?"

"If you prefer. Will you marry me?"

"Finally! I was beginning to wonder when you'd come out with it, or if we'd keep playing hide-and-seek indefinitely. We didn't see the time pass."

"It's true, the war upset our plans."

"I think the war was only an excuse. We were absorbed in our activities, swept off our feet by our passion for research. We will continue, of course. But this time together, in the same place. McGill gave me a professorship. They owed it to me! I've done enough to end this war!"

"So you have. And now it's time to think about us."

"Paul, do you have any idea of where we could get married?"

"In Paris, of course."

~ *EPILOGUE* ~

Nobel Committees are usually unanimous in their choice of recipients. At least this is generally true of sciences such as physics and chemistry.

When it comes to physiology or medicine, the decisions are sometimes controversial. This is mainly due to the fact that Alfred Nobel, in his will, had not imagined how these disciplines would evolve, nor the way in which scientists would work in laboratories of the future.

The virulent battle around the discovery of insulin perfectly illustrates this difficulty. Several individuals, perhaps five or six, had deserved that distinction. Besides Frederick Banting and John McLeod, James Collip and Charles Best should have officially shared the Nobel Prize in 1923. The clinician Walter Campbell and Romanian researcher Nicolas Paulesco could also have been associated with this extraordinary discovery. Today it is difficult for the Nobel Committee in physiology or medicine at the Karolinska Institute to comply with the wishes of Alfred Nobel. The conditions of research have changed. In the past, scientists often worked alone, and Alfred Nobel had limited the number of award recipients to a maximum of three. This sometimes gave rise to disappointment. Moreover, in the past, contact with colleagues in other countries was naturally less frequent, and access to scientific literature much more limited.

The problems that already existed in the early twentieth century are even more pronounced today. Due to the way in which research and its techniques have evolved, a scientific idea rarely originates with a single individual. It is only when an idea is mature and methodologies are fully developed to demonstrate it, that the idea becomes reality and can lead to great discoveries.

The Nobel Prizes of 2012 are a good example. The Nobel Prize in physiology or medicine, awarded to John Gurdon and Shinya Yamanaka for the reprogramming of induced pluripotent stem cells (iPS) resulted from work on stem cells; the latter are found in many tissues in our bodies, allowing them to constantly reconstitute from a very small number of genes. Similarly, the Nobel Prize in chemistry, rightly granted to Robert Lefkowitz and Brian Kobilka, could also have been awarded to researchers who had worked for years on G-protein coupled receptors. As the recipients themselves declared, their work was the logical continuation of the work honoured by Earl Sutherland's Nobel in 1971, and the Nobel of 1994 awarded to Alfred Gilman and Martin Rodbell for the discovery of the role of G proteins in signal transduction in cells.

It was only in the 1990s that G protein-coupled receptor antagonists, like those described in this novel, were developed, some to block the pathways of stress. They still have not yet been put on the market.

The development of science has been, and will always be a source of conflict, injustice and disillusionment for those who obtain the Prize and those who rightly wish for recognition of their contribution. It is also certain that the Anglo-Saxon and especially the American control of scientific journals have accentuated these conflicts. We have seen how Hans Selye, by writing and publishing in German his work on the improvement of pituitary ablation techniques, probably delayed the rapid and reproducible use of the methodology by his competitor, the Evans laboratory.

The Nobel Peace Prize, awarded by the Norwegian Academy, has always been the subject of intense criticism since politics became involved. For example, how could Theodore Roosevelt have deserved the Nobel Peace Prize more than John Monash? Though crucial to ending the First World War, the General's contribution has disappeared from collective memory, except perhaps in Australia, where a large university near Melbourne bears his name.

As for James (Bert) Collip, he distinguished himself as an outstanding scientist through his discoveries on hormones, parathyroid hormone (PTH), pituitary hormones such as adrenocorticotropic hormone (ACTH) and the thyroid stimulating hormone (TSH), as well as oestrogens and placental hormones. These pioneering works have been the subject of 250 publications. James Collip also carried out productive action for policy research in Canada. His work has made a name for the country, internationally in several disciplines, as evidenced by the work in its excellent research centres and prestigious universities all over Canada. James Collip developed relations between industrials and academic laboratories, thereby increasing the funds available for advanced research. He died in 1965 at the age of seventy-three, without obtaining the Nobel Prize.

From the Toronto group of four, Charles (Charley) Best is

the one who lived the longest. After succeeding Frederick Banting, he had his own institute, right next to that of Banting. Both institutes still exist on the campus of the University of Toronto. On the top floor, there is even a small museum where visitors can see the instruments used in the discovery of insulin. Charles Best was subsequently honoured and acclaimed all over the world. He continued to do research with great enthusiasm, discovering heparin, which prevents venous thrombosis and is still used clinically. The discovery led to his nomination for the Nobel Prize, but he did not receive it. He died in 1978.

Banting, like his colleagues, is in the Canadian 'Hall of Fame'. There is a Sir Frederick Banting Foundation in Alliston, Ontario www.bantinglegacy.ca.

Frank Macfarlane Burnet, also known as Mac, Paul's friend in Melbourne in the novel, was awarded the Nobel Prize in physiology or medicine in 1960 for his work on acquired immunological tolerance. Howard Florey, a young student at the time of the discovery of insulin, was awarded the Nobel Prize in 1945, together with Alexander Fleming and Ernst Chain for their work on penicillin.

Chemists Tadeusz Reichstein and Vladimir Proleg, in 1950 and 1975 respectively, won the Nobel Prize in their discipline for their work on hormone synthesis of adrenal steroids and the stereochemistry of molecules, as well as work on adamantane and quinine.

Jacques Monod, the French scientist, musician, resistant, politician and my professor of molecular biology at University Paris VI in the 1970s, won the Nobel Prize in physiology or medicine in 1965 with two other French scientists, André Lwoff and François Jacob, for their work on the genetic control of enzyme and virus synthesis, and the discovery of the lactose operon. He passed away in May 1976.

Nominated twenty times, Hans Selye never had the honour of receiving the Nobel Prize. Why not? Nobody knows. His research nonetheless left an indelible mark on the world of research in endocrinology, more specifically, neuro-endocrinology, the study of the relations between the nervous system and the endocrine system. Throughout the fifty-four years of his career in science, Hans Selye published over 1,700 articles and 39 books. In 1943, he had a fresco painted on his office wall showing the endocrine glands and their hormones. The fresco is still visible in the Anatomy Department at McGill University in Montreal. Hans Selye is also the 'father of stress' (see the article published in *Nature*: Vol 138, p.32, 04.07.1936). The word stress is now commonly used in our society to describe a situation of malaise, poor adjustment and its individual, societal and financial consequences. Before his death in 1982, he was no doubt delighted to see his student Roger Guillemin receive the Nobel Prize in physiology or medicine in 1977, along with Andrew Schally and Rosalyn Yalow, for the discovery of hypothalamic neuropeptides and their quantitation. This work was the direct result of the training and education that Roger Guillemin had received in Montreal under the direction of Hans Selye.

Receiving the Nobel Prize has numerous consequences on the winners. They go from being virtually unknown to public, to the status of star and thereby face many demands that often fall outside the scope of their skills. One can get a taste for the glory that invariably accompanies the Nobel Prize. But some people experience a kind of malaise and exhibit "a poor response to stress," as Hans Selye would have said.

The case of Frederick Banting speaks for itself. He was far from being a public figure. He did not communicate well, unlike John McLeod. He hated the receptions that his first wife, Marion Robertson, doted upon. It was undoubtedly his great difficulty with public speaking, as may be recalled from this book, which spurred on his quarrel with Professor McLeod. There are multiple examples of behaviours exhibited by winners of the Nobel since its establishment in 1901, discussed in the excellent sociological study by Josepha Laroche (see references).

But have you heard of Josephine Cochrane, Alva Fisher or John Chamberlain? They too would have deserved the Nobel Prize for their discoveries, those of Peace and Science combined. They invented and developed the dishwasher and washing machine, resulting in a significant decrease in conflicts between husbands and wives!

Paul Dormont, for his part in numerous discoveries, and perhaps Louise Leblanc too, for her work on nuclear power, might have obtained the Nobel Prize... if they had not merely been fictional heroes.

~ *REFERENCES* ~

ARZALIER Francis and NICOLI Francette. *Jean Nicoli : de la colonie à la Corse en résistance*. Albiana, 2003.

BARR Murray and EOSSITER Roger L. *James J. Bertram Collip*. Royal Society of London, p. 235-267, 1973.

BEST Henry B. M. Margaret and Charley. *The Personal story of Dr. Charles Best, the Co-discoverer of Insulin*. DundurnPress, 2003.

BIZIER Hélène-Andrée. *L'Université de Montréal: la quête du savoir*. Libre Expression, 1993.

BLISS Michael. *Banting: A biography*. University of Toronto Press, 1992.

BLISS Michael. *The discovery of Insulin*. University of Toronto Press, Canada, 2007.

CALLAHAN William R. *The Banting Enigma*. Flanker Press, St. John's, Nfld, Canada, 2005.

CANADA: un siècle 1867-1967. Bureau fédéral de la statistique, Ottawa, Canada, 1967.

CASTA François. *Homme de Dieu, homme de guerre*. L'esprit du livre, 2009.

CONANT Jennet. *The Irregulars*. Simon & Schuster, New York, 2008.

DEBRE Patrice. *Jacques Monod*. Flammarion, Paris, 1996.

ETTINGER G. Harold. *Medical Research in Canada During The War*. Presentation at the Saturday Club, December 18, 1943.

FRIEDLAND Martin L. *The University of Toronto: a history*. University of Toronto Press, 2002.

FROST Stanley B. *McGill University, vols. 1 and 2.* McGill-Queen's University Press, 1984 and 1985.

GAMBIEZ Fernand. *Libération de la Corse*. Hachette, 1973.

GREY Jeffrey. *Histoire militaire de l'Australie*. Cambridge University Press, 2000.

GRIFFI Toussaint and PREZIOSI Laurent. *Première mission en Corse occupée*. L'Harmattan, 1988.

LAROCHE Josepha. *Les Prix Nobel: sociologie d'une élite transnationale*. Ed Liber, Montréal, 2012.

LI, Alison. *J.B. Collip and the Development of Medical Research in Canada*. McGill-Queen's University Press, 2003.

MONOD Jacques. *Le hasard et la nécessité. Essai sur la philosophie naturelle de la biologie moderne*. Ed du Seuil, 1970.

MORTON, Desmond. *Histoire militaire du Canada*. Ed Athena, Outremont, Québec, 2007.

PERRY, Roland. *Monash: the Outsider who Won a War*. Random House, Australia, 2004.

ROSTENE, William and FREU Julien. *L'Héritage de Paul. Paul Bert, l'homme des possibles*. L'Harmattan, 2012.

RUBIN, Ronald. P. *A Brief History of Great Discoveries in Pharmacology: in celebration of the centennial anniversary of the founding of the American Society of Pharmacology and Experimental Therapeutics*. Pharmacological 59: 289-359, 2007.

RUSSELL, Kenneth. *The Melbourne Medical School, 1862-1962*. Melbourne

Scientific papers and correspondence of Hans Selye. Hans Selye Foundation (P0359), University of Montreal.

Scientific papers and correspondence of Frederick Banting, James Collip, John McLeod and Charles Best.Thomas Fisher Rare Book Library.University of Toronto (entered in the register of the World Memory of UNESCO in June 2013). MS. Coll 76 and MS. 285 Coll.

The Banting Homestead Heritage Park, Alliston, Canada. www.bantinglegacy.ca

La Corse dans la seconde guerre mondiale. Ed Albiana.

The Nobel Foundation. http: //www.nobelprize.org

~ *ACKNOWLEDGMENTS* ~

The authors wish to thank all those who have supported the idea of writing a novel inspired by some of the lesser-known chapters in the history of science. These people from all over the world, with their knowledge and practical support, have played a crucial role in the accomplishment of this work. Many thanks to:

In Australia:
Professor Iain Clarke, Monash University, Clayton
Dr. Michael McKinley, University of Melbourne

In Canada:
Trudi and Bob Banting, The Banting Homestead Heritage Park, Alliston, Ontario
Janna Ramsay Best, Sudbury, Ontario
Professor Michael Bliss, University of Toronto
Jean Dansereau, Montreal
Luba Frastacky and Jennifer Toews, Thomas Fisher Rare Book Library, University of Toronto
Monique Généreux, International Relations, Laval University, Quebec

Josée Lalonde and Roger Poitras, Quebec

James Lambert, Archivist Laval University, Quebec

Michèle Richard, Stanstead, Quebec

David Sadleir, President of the Banting Homestead Heritage Park, Alliston, Ontario

Dr. Milagros Salas-Prato, Selye Foundation, Montreal

Monique and Michel Voyer Champagne, Archivists University of Montreal

Dr. Christopher Yp, University of Toronto

Dr. Alain Beaudet, Head Canadian Institute of Health Research, Ottawa

In the USA:

Professor Roger Guillemin, Nobel Prize in Physiology or Medicine

Nancy McEwen, New York

In France:

Ange Barbagelata, Pietrosella, Corsica

Professor Etienne-Emile Baulieu, Paris

Caroline, Marie-Lou and George, Le Belvedere, Coti-Chiavari, Corsica

Dr. François Casabianca, Corte, Corsica

Julien Freu, Toulouse

Dr. Christian Grimaud, Pietrosella, Corsica

Dr. Caroline Leriche, Sanofi, Paris

Marie-Josée Milleliri, Corte, Corsica

Dr. Andrée Piekarski, Paris

Sophie Verdeil, Levie, Corsica

Many thanks to Alison Strayer for her masterful English translation of *Les Caprices du Nobel.*

Also to Alain Bekerman, whose support made the translation possible, and to the Association pour la Recherche sur le Diabète et les Insuffisances Cérébrales (AREDIC).

Finally, Professor Peter Wise, Professor Jo Herbert, Professor Iain Clarke and Michael Vines who made pertinent suggestions on the last version of the English manuscript.

~ *ABOUT THE AUTHORS* ~

William Rostène is an Emeritus research director at INSERM and works at the Vision Institute - University Pierre et Marie Curie in Paris. An internationally renowned expert in neuroscience, he has published hundreds of articles in prestigious journals such as Nature, PNAS, Journal of Neuroscience, Neuroendocrinology... He is president of the Société de Biologie and co-author with Julien Freu of an historical novel entitled L'Héritage de Paul (Paul's Legacy), first published in 2007, followed by a second edition in 2012 by L'Harmattan, Publ. He also writes scientific books for children (Le Pommier Publ).

Hélène Rostène is a high school English professor in Paris, France.

Lightning Source UK Ltd.
Milton Keynes UK
UKOW01f0627210218
318251UK00001B/5/P